"Hey, I wasn't the one ironing letterman jackets all night." I took out the folder of notes I had made the night before.

We worked until her father nicely asked me to leave.[12]

She gave me her usual you're-my-best-friend-so-it's-so-harmless-to-be-close-to-you hug. I just hugged her back in that I'm-perfectly-content-to-only-be-friends way and headed home.

As I walked down Kimball Street, I thought of all the things I forgot to tell Beth tonight. About the links we could set up from Larry's home page. About how spring was only a few weeks away. About my conversation with Flip-Off Phillips that morning.

And oh yeah, Beth, one more thing.

Did I forget to mention I was Larry?

(I'm not much of a detail person.)[13]

---

[12] If standing at the top of the stairs and coughing is considered nice.

[13] Okay, so I strung you along a little—big deal. Had to make sure you were with me first.

The Gospel
ACCORDING
TO LARRY

JANET TASHJIAN

LAUREL-LEAF BOOKS

Published by
Dell Laurel-Leaf
an imprint of
Random House Children's Books
a division of Random House, Inc.
New York

Visit us on the Web! www.randomhouse.com/teens

Educators and librarians, for a variety of teaching tools, visit us at
www.randomhouse.com/teachers

ISBN: 0-440-23792-0

RL: 6.0

Reprinted by arrangement with Henry Holt and Company, LLC

Printed in the United States of America

May 2003

1 0 9 8 7 6 5

OPM

For Josh . . .

(and Larry)

wherever you are

A Note to the Reader

While I was waiting in line at the local grocery store, a young man approached me and asked me for the time. I told him ten past four—I remember it distinctly—and continued emptying my carriage onto the conveyor belt. He hovered around the store's exit and approached me again as I left. He held a copy of my first novel, *Tru Confessions.*

"Aren't you a writer?"

I told him I was.

"I've got a great story for you," he said.

"Oh, yeah?" I pushed the shopping cart toward my car. "You know who the best person to tell your story is?"

He shook his head.

"You."

He smiled, then offered me a bundle of typed pages held together with twine. It looked like a thesis but smelled like the bottom of the earth. I didn't take it.

"There are lots of great publishing houses out there. I'd start in New York. You can always go the agent route too." I finished loading the groceries into my car, then gave him my best nice-to-meet-you smile.

"You don't understand," he said. "I'm not even supposed to *be* here."

I closed the trunk and looked at him. Blond hair—half grown out into its natural brown—serious eyes, slight build, peaceful smile. Seventeen, eighteen years old. He looked vaguely familiar.

"This has to get published." He pressed the papers into my hand. "I don't know what else to do."

He stood on one leg, the other one bent and tucked against it. It was a yoga position my son and I practiced all the time. "Tree pose?" I asked.

He nodded. "I'm trying to stay balanced."

"Aren't we all."

He seemed completely unself-conscious. "I just came back from Walden Pond. You ever been there?"

"Many times."

He pulled the paperback *Walden* from his back pocket and started to read. " 'To be a philosopher is not merely to have subtle thoughts, nor even to found a school, but so to love wisdom as to live according to its dictates, a life of simplicity, independence, magnanimity, and trust.' " He looked at me, eyes shining. "Isn't that the best?"

What do you say to a kid standing on one leg while quoting Thoreau? I told him I'd read his manuscript.

"I set it up like a term paper," he said. "Typed it on an old manual typewriter in the woods. Then I pulled stuff from the Web, added some biblical quotes . . ." He smiled. "It'll all make sense. You'll see."

He placed his foot firmly on the ground. "If you decide not to help me, I'll understand."

I asked how I should contact him.

"That's impossible," he said. "I'll contact you."

On the drive home, I skimmed through the pages on my lap. I sat in my driveway and continued to read, unfazed by the gallon of ice cream melting in my trunk.

I *thought* he looked familiar. I raced back to the grocery store to find him, but he had already gone.

By the time he called the next day, I had read his entire manuscript.

"Well?" he asked. (His anticipation reminded me so much of my own, waiting to get my first novel published.)

I told him I had another project I was working on but thought his version of the story was important and needed to be told. I asked my editor, Christy, if she'd be interested in publishing the manuscript. After reading it, she was.

Josh also gave me a disk with photos he'd taken; we placed them throughout the book. The epilogue was my idea, to add another perspective.

Working on the book, I sometimes found Josh's story inspirational; other times it seemed eerie and devoid of meaning. In my research, I found some people who said Josh suffered from bipolar disorder or ADHD; one teacher even said he thought Josh had an acute "messiah complex." All I know is, the young man I met several times over the course of a month seemed perfectly normal. But don't go by me—I sit in a room and make up stories all day.

When my editor mailed me the galleys a few months ago, I talked to Josh for the last time. "You realize if we publish this, people will know you're still alive," I said. "The whole mess might start up again."

His voice sounded calm and rational. "It's really important for me to be honest right now," he said. "I just want to write about the truth."

I tried to reach him later to give him some copies of the book, but he'd disappeared.

Again.

This is his story.

Janet Tash

The Gospel
ACCORDING TO LARRY

The Gospel According to Larry—

in my own words

by

Josh Swensen

PART ONE

"This is the disciple which testifieth
of these things, and wrote these things:
and we know that his testimony is true."

St. John 21:24

"I haven't enjoyed a rant this much since Thoreau,"[1] Beth said. "We *need* people stirring up the way we think about things."

My best friend, Beth, was trying to talk me into forming a Larry study group with her. His Web site—www.thegospelaccordingtolarry.com—received hundreds of hits a day, mostly from teens and college students. No one knew Larry's identity, and that conjecture alone was the source of several companion Web sites. Many kids at school were fans, but Beth was rabid.

"Josh, I know neither one of us has ever joined a club in our life," she said. "But that's precisely why we should."

I tried to listen to the details of her story, I really did, but there is something

---

[1] Henry David Thoreau wrote *Walden* and *Civil Disobedience*. We had to read them for English last semester—very New England—nature is good, materialism is bad. Beth ate it up with a spoon.

about Beth's mouth that gets in the way of paying attention to its contents.[2] She often wore a certain brown lipstick and outlined the edges of her lips with this pencil she carried in her bag. Every time she talked, it was like this pale chocolate snowcone staring up at me, waiting to be eaten. I've been in love with her since sixth grade, but she didn't have a clue.

"I'll help you with the club," I said. "But just so the two of us can bag all the meetings and laugh at the other people who show up."

She wasn't amused. "This isn't a joke. Someone is finally talking about the things I've been saying all along, and I think it's important to help spread the word. Are you in or are you out?"

"Of course I'm in. I can't let you do this on your own. Next thing I know you'll be running for prom queen or something."

She punched me in the arm, her usual form of affection. "Hey, why don't you help me at the store this afternoon? We're having a run on shovels."

---

[2] She would HATE me for saying this with her don't-objectify-me rant. Protest all you want, Beth—it's the truth.

Beth's father's hardware store had been our work/tree house/summer camp since grammar school. Sorting the nuts and bolts, counting the different lightbulbs, shoveling the woodchips into wheelbarrows had never seemed like a job to either of us. The small store prided itself on carrying everything a homeowner could need, but for a loner like me it was a nonthreatening way to be a part of the community without too much social pressure. I told Beth I'd meet her there at four.

For a brief moment I pretended we were a couple, not snowbound outside Boston, but romping through the Caribbean surf—tan and in love. My fantasy shattered, however, when she waved goodbye and headed across the cafeteria to Todd Terrific—a new jock she was obsessed with. Can someone please explain to me how this preoccupation with dopey athletes happens even to headstrong young women who work in hardware stores and score 1350s on their SATs? Beth, what are you doing to me? Life was cruel and unfair—what did this Larry guy have to say about *that*?

The rest of school went by like the movie *Groundhog Day*, where Bill Murray wakes up and every day is the same, down to the last boring

details. Even when something new did happen—
fire drill, substitute teacher—it was still
just a giant yawn in the storyline. To keep
myself amused during study hall, I invented a
new alphabet based on the sense of smell.[3]

At home that night, I booted up my laptop
and logged on. I checked my e-mail, then the
small portfolio of stocks my mother left me
when she died. I made one last online stop: to
Larry. I wondered if Beth was doing the same
thing at the same time—an unrequited cyber-
date.

The Larry logo filled the screen—a peace
sign with a dove, a floppy disk, a planet, and
a plug inside each of its four sections. I
scrolled down through several photographs to
comments people had written that day: puljohn
posted a new link to Adbusters. Toejam ranted
about Larry's last sermon, calling it bril-
liantly flawed. I was in the middle of reading
his argument when Peter knocked quickly, then
stuck his head in my room.

"Want some leftover pizza?"

---

[3] I also wrote a skit for Monty Python, in case they ever
wanted to reunite, then drew sketches for the Gumby art
project I was working on. Got to keep busy, I always say.

My stepfather was the ultimate businessman; even in his terrycloth robe and slippers with the squashed heels, he could command his advertising consulting firm from the brink of failure to unbridled success. He had the whole sales thing down—the firm handshake, the warm smile, the good listening. It was the real Peter, not put on, like lots of other guys at his company.

He looked over my shoulder and checked out the screen.

"I've heard about this Larry," he said. "Some guy bashing our culture online. Anonymous coward."

"Some people think it's one of the big televangelists trying to reach the teen market. Or maybe it's a bored housewife in the suburbs looking for something to do."

Peter shook his head. "Probably some hacker trying to make a name for himself."

"I'll add that to the list of hypotheses," I said.

"You do that." He handed me a slice of pizza on a paper towel. "Dinner at Katherine's tomorrow. That okay with you?"

"Sure. Great." Katherine was my stepfather's girlfriend who had been putting on the full-court press to be the next Mrs. Swensen. I didn't have the nerve to tell Peter I found her as interesting as a bag of rice.

Peter closed the door and headed downstairs to his office. I browsed the Larry archives, then printed out the latest sermon to prepare for Beth tomorrow.

SERMON #93

Slip on your Gap jeans, your Nike T-shirt, your Reeboks—or maybe even your Cons if you think that makes you cool and ironic in a Kurt Cobain kind of way. Grab your Adidas backpack, ride to school on your Razor, drink your Poland Spring, eat your PowerBar, write a paper on your iMac, slip on your Ralph Lauren windbreaker. Buy the latest CD from Tower, check the caller ID to see who's on the phone, eat your Doritos, drink your Coke. Stare at the TV till you're stupefied.

Is there any time of the day when we're not being used and abused by the advertising companies? Can we have an inch of free space, do you mind? Some

ambitious kids rent their head space—
the outside, not the inside (although
the inside space is certainly emptier)—
to local companies by shaving ads into
their hair for all their friends to
see. It's just a matter of time before
corporations figure out a way to sell
you stuff while you're sleeping. Maybe
some kind of vitamin that releases
visual and sonic enzymes that run like a
ticker tape through your dreams—ALL THE
LATEST RELEASES NOW AT BLOCKBUSTER . . .
CHEESIER NACHOS AT CHILI'S . . . BY THE
WAY, YOU'RE SNORING. . . .

Am I the only one who sees the irony
of sitting in lit class reading 1984,
having a discussion of Big Brother
watching out for us like it's some time
way in the future? Some science fiction
nightmare that's never really going to
happen? Hel-lo? Our lives couldn't be
more dictated by the corporations if
they gave our schools A/V equipment in
exchange for making us watch commercials in class.

Oh yeah, they do that already.
Never mind.

Good thing Peter hadn't hung around for that one. By two A.M., I had fourteen pages of notes for the new Larry club.[4] When I added up all the things I'd done for Beth over the years, I figured it was more effort than they put into developing the last space shuttle.

And completely and totally worth it.

---

[4] I'd help Beth for as long as possible, providing I could leave the club as soon as it got weird. Too many people at the same time usually sends me heading for the hills.

Joining anything was not my usual thing—by a long shot. It's like that show *Survivor.* I read in the paper that 50 million people watched it last night—talk about a reason *not* to watch something. I don't know about you, but if 50 million people are doing something, I want to be doing something else—*big* time.

My stepfather's girlfriend calls me quirky, but most of the kids in my school would probably just call me weird. I'm used to it, though; it's always been that way. I mean, when you're sitting in third grade wearing a paper pyramid on your head to see if the rays of energy will help you concentrate, you're getting some kids looking at you like you're cuckoo. The good news was—I never cared. Never came home crying, never worried, "Oh, gosh, what will the other kids think?" Just plain old oblivious. There's something to be said about ignorance being bliss.[5]

When my mother was still alive, she used to threaten the principal for more services—extra tutors, more challenging work. "He's seven years old with an eighth-grade math level. You're wasting his time making him add two plus two!" she'd yell. "I'll homeschool him, I swear!"

Yeah, Mom. Sure. Maybe after a handful of Prozac and a lobotomy. God rest her soul, she was a tireless advocate for me, but she could sit still about as much as I could. I can picture her homeschooling me now, the two of us spelling vocabulary words as we rolled down the hill behind the cemetery. She was a character—loud voice, loud music, loud clothes. So much fun. Until the ovarian cancer—much less fun after that.

For most of my life with her, the stimulation level was high, and that's always been a turn-on for me. I didn't crawl or walk; one day I just got up and ran. My very first word— yelled, not spoken from my carseat as we cruised down the highway—was *FASTER!* And once

---

[5] Not too much, of course, but something.

I got hold of numbers, forget about it. There's a home video of me, probably about two years old, sitting on one of those jumpy seats in the kitchen. I'm in front of the refrigerator with colored magnetic numbers doing equations.[6] My mother's talking to one of her girlfriends while she's taping me, saying, "When most babies want formula, they're not talking about math."

But it wasn't just numbers; it was learning in general that excited me. I'd go through phases where I devoured any information about the Civil War, Tibetan Buddhism, alpine mountaineering, and planting a perennial garden.[7] The usual kid activities like baseball and soccer didn't interest me. I remember having huge fights with my mother while she held open the screen door and forced me to play outside with the neighborhood kids. "If you don't go out and play with Karl and Bryan right now, there'll be no science homework after dinner!"

"Don't even think about taking my biology away!"

---

[6] I swear to God, this is true—two years old.

[7] I don't know if you know this, but you can lose a lot of friends talking nonstop about peat moss.

"Josh, get out there and get some fresh air, or so help me God, I'm bringing those math books back to the library!"

She'd boot me out the door kicking and screaming. As the years went by, I still preferred to work on my laptop in my hammock swing than to be at the high school Super Bowl.

Beth used to call me "The Wizard," like I was some overgrown Harry Potter. She thought I just twirled around, wasting time, visiting various dictionary sites to look up words like *napiform* (it means turnip-shaped, but you know that).

"You are NOT the average seventeen-year-old," she told me once. "But then again, you weren't the average fifteen- or twelve-year-old either."

I had to agree with her there.

It's very simple, really. I've only wanted one thing my whole life—to contribute, to help make the world a better place. It sounds amazingly corny, but pushing civilization forward has always been my highest priority. Not with more technology, not with more money, but with more ideas, more meaning. When we studied Darwin last year, his ideas burned off the page. All of us, evolving, moving forward, consciously or not. It's probably what was in

18

the back of my mind when I moved those plastic numbers across the refrigerator; it's what's on my mind as I type this now.

If Larry was a way to delve into life's deeper meaning, then count me in.

Beth made a list of all the kids in our homeroom and who they had been in a past life. We
passed the list back and forth filling in the
blanks—Jack Furtado, Victorian cellist; Laura
Newman, Russian cosmonaut—until the bell rang.

Out in the hall, my enthusiasm pinned Beth
to her locker. "You're right! Everything Larry
wrote about on his Web site had something to do
with my life."

"Didn't I tell you?" She couldn't have been
happier.

"When I thought about what a consumer glutton my stepfather's girlfriend was, Larry wrote
about shopaholics. When I missed my mother, he
talked about attachment. It was uncanny!" I
didn't want to lay it on too thick.

Beth's lips shone like a hot mocha coffee. "He
puts into words exactly what we're thinking."
She corrected herself immediately. "He or she."

"But what's with the photos?" I asked. "Are we supposed to guess Larry's identity?"

"Larry has less than eighty possessions. He posts them on his Web site, a few at a time, daring people to guess who he is. Right now, everyone's clueless. I mean, what can you tell from a pen and a hairbrush?"

"Maybe you'll be lucky and the next clue will be his—"

"Or her—"

"License."

Beth smiled. "I'm sure Larry's saving that one for last."

I asked her if she wanted to come over later and talk about my ideas for the club.

She frowned. "I can't. I have to study for that calculus test."

Beth was a lot of things—gorgeous, smart, determined. She also was a terrible liar. I stared her down.

"Okay, I promised I'd help my father with inventory."

I kept staring.

"Damn it, Josh. I told Todd I'd help him clean his basement tonight. Okay?"

"Could you please explain how someone as committed to personal growth as you are can vacuum the basement of the class cretin just because she thinks she's in love with him?"

"I don't want to hear it," Beth barked back. "There's no one more inconsistent than you. You're a computer geek who hikes in the woods for days. You hate to buy things, yet you always go to Bloomingdale's!"

"That's different. But forget it, you made your point."

She was just gearing up. "Look, you're my best friend. We've been bailing each other out since grade school. But not everyone wants to go through life being a hermit living in the world of ideas." She made quotation marks with her fingers when she said the word *ideas*. It was one of the only things Beth did that drove me out of my mind.

She finally got around to sputtering out the truth about Todd. "He's the only cool guy who's ever liked me. I know he can act like a jerk, but do you mind if I let his popularity rub off on me for a while?"

For some reason the bare-bones honesty of her plea only fueled my growing sense of annoyance. "I'm out of here." I made those fake quotation marks around the word *out*, then walked toward lit class. I could feel her behind me even before she spun me around to face her.

"I hate fighting with you," she said. "Hate it, hate it, hate it."

We stood silently for a few minutes.

"It's just that Todd has to have the basement cleaned by the weekend or he can't play. I'm trying to have some school spirit for once. Plus, he knows I'm really good at organizing things. . . ."

I wanted to tell her those skills might be put to better use than placing football and basketball trophies in chronological order, but I held my tongue. Instead I told her I had lots to do, tons to do, was way too busy to deal with this paltry exchange. I shuffled away as nonchalantly as someone in deep despair could shuffle. My anxiety around Beth could be traced to one thing—I was never included in the endlessly rotating list of guys she had crushes on. Sam, Daniel, Andy, Speedy McDermott, Jack, now Todd. But never, ever me. If the choice were a two-week exciting vacation in Europe with me or helping Todd clean his basement, I knew, sadly, what Beth's choice would be.

Next stop in my fun-filled day: guidance with Ms. Phillips. I tried to rally myself for the occasion by doing some standing push-ups against my locker.

I hadn't even sat down when Ms. Phillips got to the point. "Have you thought about your major, Josh?"

Ms. Phillips had the terrible habit of pushing her glasses up her nose with her middle finger. She did it so often, everyone in school called her Flip-Off Phillips.

I played with the zipper of my bookbag, then realized I was not giving her my full attention—Larry's Sermon #22. I looked her in the eyes. "I was thinking about philosophy. You know, the meaning of life—that sort of thing."

"From the point of view of someone who likes to read, likes to think, like you do, it's a good choice," she said. "But you realize the job prospects are pretty slim."

"I'm thinking after the Depression, after the Apocalypse, there'll be lots of positions for people with depth and vision."

She crinkled up her nose, her glasses fell, and she flipped me the bird again. "Josh, I'm not sure it makes sense to plan a career based on an apocalypse. What if there isn't one?"

"Then I guess I'm screwed." I flashed her a big smile so she couldn't yell at me for the language.

"I suppose I'm being too materialistic," she said. "Studying philosophy at Princeton is a fine and worthy choice."

I wasn't sure Ms. Phillips's revelation came less from my sales pitch than it did from the fact that it was ten to eleven and she was dying for a cigarette before her next appointment. I decided to let her off the nicotine hook; I gathered up my things and headed for the door.

I've had a soft spot in my heart for Ms. Phillips since last year, when I spotted her e-mail address in her office and started up a chatty Internet conversation with her as a forty-year-old bachelor from Portland.[8] After months of quiet online flirtation, I invited her to meet me at the Borders coffee shop, only to watch her from the cookbook section. She waited more than two hours and three cappuccinos before she went home. (*That* I felt bad about. Ms. Phillips was usually tough as nails; I never thought she'd fall that hard.)

I decided to skip the rest of the day; the recurring vision of Beth dressed up like Snow

---

[8] I don't care what anyone says—I was not going through her desk.

White singing as she swept Todd Terrific's basement was more than I could endure. I grabbed my camera from my locker and opted to check in with my mother instead.

When my stepfather visited Mom, he headed for the cemetery. I—who knew her much better than he did—headed for somewhere that captured her spirit more than a pasture full of granite headstones.

The makeup counter at Bloomingdale's.

I slogged through the slush, then grabbed the bus to Chestnut Hill. Ever since we lived in the Boston area, my mother had dragged me here once a month.

The waft of perfumes hit me like a surge of memories. I plopped down in the tall seat at the Chanel counter. I think it's safe to say I was the only person in that department sitting in the lotus position.

"Hello, Joshie. How's it going?" Marlene the Beauty Doctor has been working here for more than twenty years. With her shiny helmet of dyed black hair and dark eyebrows penciled in for the ones she lost years ago, she was Mom's favorite salesperson.

"It's slow, so you can sit. If I get a client, you know the drill."

I saluted, then leaned back to hang with Mom.

My mother bailed on her wealthy parents' expectations as soon as she hit college. Instead of following in their Wall Street footsteps, she hitchhiked cross-country, worked tirelessly for civil rights, and made some bad choices in men. One thing from her Grosse Pointe background she couldn't walk away from, however, was her fondness for upscale moisturizers and creams. She used to spend hours trying to look like she wore no makeup at all. She experimented with pencils and powders like a mad scientist but always looked the same to me. I can remember perching on this stool as a preschooler watching Marlene hand Mom tube after tube of lipstick. Mom would ask me which color I preferred, consider my answer, then buy whichever one she wanted anyway.

I waited till Marlene rang someone up at the other end of the counter before I started talking.

"Okay, Mom, in a nutshell—Beth is cleaning Todd's basement, Peter is dragging me to another lasagna dinner at Katherine's, and I'm nowhere closer to changing the world."

A woman with a leopard-print hat eyed me as she walked by.

"I just feel like I'm waiting for my life to begin, that I've wasted seventeen years. Then

27

what? Four years at Princeton? How does that help move civilization forward?"

"You want to see our deep-pore cleaning mask?" Marlene inquired.

I nodded. Whenever Marlene's boss circled by, I pretended I was a paying customer.

"You ask me, you make it too hard on yourself. Stop worrying about civilization. Worry about staying out of trouble, making nice friends," Marlene said.

She rubbed the mask onto my face in small circles.

"I have nice friends," I answered. "Well, one nice friend."

"One nice friend is all you need." Marlene watched her boss get on the escalator, then wiped off my mask with a tissue.

"Here." She gathered up tiny bottles of free samples, put them in a small bag with handles, and gave it to me. "You come back anytime."

I could see Marlene eyeing a potential customer hovering over the nail polish. I saluted again and left.

In the shoe department, I tried on four pairs of sneakers, three pairs of loafers, and five pairs of boots before the salesperson deserted me. I circled by the makeup counter on my way out.

"Mom?" I asked.

A fiftyish woman in fishnets turned around, then went back to what she was doing.

"Mom, you'll help me, right? With the whole change-the-world thing?"

Then I did what I always did when I needed an answer from my mother. I listened for the very next word someone said. A businessman talking on his cell phone provided her response.

"Yes!" he said into the phone. "Of course I will."

My grin spread ear to ear.

When I said, "Thanks, Mom," the woman in fishnets turned around again. I tipped my woolen hat her way and headed out of the store.

LARRY ITEM #8

Peter's girlfriend Katherine had a Humpty Dumpty fetish. She collected anything poor Mr. Dumpty had affixed himself to—salt and pepper shakers, cookie jars, puzzles, mailboxes, light switches, vases, bookends—you get the idea. Last Christmas, she gave Peter a Humpty Dumpty tie with clumsy Humpty tumbling down the front of it.[9]

Katherine was forty pounds overweight, always smiling like the poster woman for Fat, Dumb, and Happy jeans.[10] She laughed nervously after everything we said and was putting in so much effort to being liked that once in a while I actually found myself rooting for her.

---

[9] She gave me a skateboard with *Humpty* written across it in lightning-bolt letters. It frightened me so much, I buried it under a stack of newspapers in the garage, then ended up giving it to the kid next door.

[10] Did I just say that? Horrible. Better read Larry's tolerance sermon again.

"Ah, lasagna. My favorite." Peter dug into the casserole dish like it was the first meal he'd had in months.[11]

"Very nice," I said. I'd told her fifty times I don't eat meat, but somehow that never seemed important enough to register on her radar screen. I filled my plate with lots of garlic bread and tomato sauce.

I'm not sure if Peter was really interested in the zany anecdote Katherine filled our airspace with—something about mixed-up files at work and her crazy boss—or if he just pretended she was a client. I don't know how she did it, but the conversation ended up where it always did—at eBay, and all the wonderful Humpty bargains Katherine was bidding on. I excused myself as soon as possible, saying I had lots of homework to do.

As I walked into the cold night air, I banged my hand against the side of my head to empty out the cascade of Katherine's gibberish. By Porter Street, I could almost hear my own thoughts again.

It's not like I was trying to walk by

---

[11] He and I are both better cooks than Katherine. And besides, she made lasagna every time we came over.

Beth's; my feet somehow ended up there. Just in time to catch her running up her driveway.

"I thought you were dusting Todd's collection of medals tonight."

"Give it a rest, Josh."

I decided to lay off the topic until she felt like talking. We sat on her front steps and watched the flickering Christmas lights the Petersons should have taken down months ago.

"I hate to admit you may be right," she began. "Todd definitely doesn't appreciate me."

"That's a giant duh."

She shivered. "I'll die if I end up being one of those women on talk shows complaining about their lives."

"I'll start a fight from the audience so the ratings will be high," I added.

"I could never have a normal conversation like this with Todd," she said. "I don't know why."

Let's see . . . because he's a moron, because he thinks memorizing football plays is more important to the planet than physics or kindness? I kept my mouth shut and stared straight ahead at the Petersons' lights.

"Oh, I almost forgot." I opened my pack and took out the gift bag from Bloomingdale's.

"You visited your mom today? I wondered where you were fifth period."

Her long fingers removed the items from the tissue paper. "Ooh, I like this." She rubbed some moisturizer on her hand.

A war erupted inside me—*please* try on the lipstick, *don't* try on the lipstick—on the one hand, I wanted any excuse to stare at those lips of hers; on the other, I needed to sleep tonight.

She wanted to torture me, of course. On went the lipstick.

"Is it too dark?" she asked.

I could feel her breath as well as see it. Her lips looked like ripe juicy plums hanging on a tree. I shrugged and told her it looked okay.

"I'm not sure about this," she said. "Larry's latest sermon really got to me—about wasting money on stuff we don't need."

"Well, it was free, if that makes you feel any better."

"As a matter of fact, it does," she said. "Want to go log on?"

I followed her down to the basement, which was strewn with clothes and CDs.

"Why don't you see if Todd will reciprocate? His basement couldn't have been any worse than this."

34

"Yeah, right. He's on his way over now."

Luckily there was no chance in hell of Todd actually doing anything resembling manual labor, so I had Beth to myself for a few hours.

She clicked on her Favorite Places and pulled up Larry's sermon. While she read the latest installment, I picked up her Magic 8 Ball and asked a question—Would Beth like Larry's new sermon? Would it resonate with her? I shook the ball, then turned it over. "My Sources Say No." I may not have magic powers, but I bet you're wrong this time, Mr. 8 Ball.

"Josh, you've got to see this."

I put down the not-so-magic Magic 8 Ball and joined her at the desk.

"Didn't I tell you? It's like he writes things just for you, no matter what you're thinking. Look."

I dragged over a chair and read the latest from Larry.

SERMON #97

I've written a lot about the crap we fill our lives with—possessions that tie us down, that only distract us from who we are trying to become. But what about the people we surround ourselves with? Are they people who ignite our passions, who spur us to greater self-mastery? Are your relationships full of meaning, or are you just going through the motions? Don't you want to dig a little deeper, reach another level? Or are we all just looking for the easy, the convenient? The people we choose to spend our lives with are the people who share our journey—are you surrounded by crewmates or pirates who hijack your time?

"It's spooky," she said. "So me and Todd."

"Yeah, I'm sure Larry was thinking of you two when he wrote it," I answered.

"I'm serious. There's no 'there' there. It's over."

I shrugged in agreement, but my brain bounced between anticipation and fantasy.

"Besides, he eats meat! I can smell it on his breath. It's disgusting." She jumped up and put her hands on her hips, determined. "Back to more important things. Let's get going on the Larry club."

"Hey, I wasn't the one ironing letterman jackets all night." I took out the folder of notes I had made the night before.

We worked until her father nicely asked me to leave.[12]

She gave me her usual you're-my-best-friend-so-it's-so-harmless-to-be-close-to-you hug. I just hugged her back in that I'm-perfectly-content-to-only-be-friends way and headed home.

As I walked down Kimball Street, I thought of all the things I forgot to tell Beth tonight. About the links we could set up from Larry's home page. About how spring was only a few weeks away. About my conversation with Flip-Off Phillips that morning.

And oh yeah, Beth, one more thing.

Did I forget to mention I was Larry?

(I'm not much of a detail person.)[13]

---

[12] If standing at the top of the stairs and coughing is considered nice.

[13] Okay, so I strung you along a little—big deal. Had to make sure you were with me first.

PART TWO

"He that findeth his life shall lose it:
and he that loseth his life for my
sake shall find it."

St. Matthew 10:39

The Web site started out as most of my projects do—as a way not to be bored, a way to create something interesting out of nothing. Also, it was that holiday juggernaut that starts with Halloween, gains steam over Thanksgiving, and comes to a roaring crescendo with Christmas and New Year. The commercialism had reached an all-time high last year, and I felt a desperate need to rebel. Especially with Mom not here, creating the site was a way to distract myself during that torturous and overwhelming time.[14]

I designed the graphics, set up the Web site using my cell phone as the modem so the line couldn't be traced.[15] I could have done the whole webcam hey-look-at-me thing, but even online my privacy was crucial.

---

[14] It hardly dented the sadness.

[15] I got the phone from an ad in the back of a magazine and registered it to a post office box.

This all came at a time when I was designing a series of biblical action figures—for no other reason than my own entertainment, of course.[16] So I called the site The Gospel According to Larry—Larry being the most un-biblical name I could think of.

At first it was funny—just two or three hits a day—lonely Internet nomads with nothing better to do than read the rantings of another spiritual pilgrim. The comments were mostly positive, and some of the arguments were stim-ulating, so I began to stay up later and later to put more time into my sermons. Someone even posted an article from a local newspaper about the site. Reading that was a hundred times more gratifying than my early acceptance letter to Princeton, believe me.

People started e-mailing Larry, asking who he or she was. One day I had the idea of pho-tographing my possessions,[17] scanning them, and posting them to the Web site. Would it be possible to track down an anonymous person ANYWHERE IN THE WORLD by the things he or she

---

[16] My favorites were Sampson and Delilah. She came with scis-sors, and his hair could actually be removed.

[17] The subject of my stuff needs its own chapter; I'll do that next.

owned? The question intrigued me. I made a bet with myself that I could photograph each item in such a way that no one could track me down.

It was a Catch-22. I was happy that what I did was interesting to others, but because Larry's identity was unknown, I couldn't take any credit for the phenomenon, couldn't use it on my resume, or more importantly, brag about it to someone like Beth. I could, I suppose, but there's something pretty slimy about a philosopher seeking attention for personal gain.[18]

So I found myself in the awkward position of starting my own fan club. It was a routine almost worthy of the Python troupe, or maybe just the Three Stooges. The irony and just plain weirdness of it invigorated me, and I spent the next hour sorting through the photographs of my possessions, deciding which one to post the next day.

---

[18] Witness the televangelists if you don't believe me.

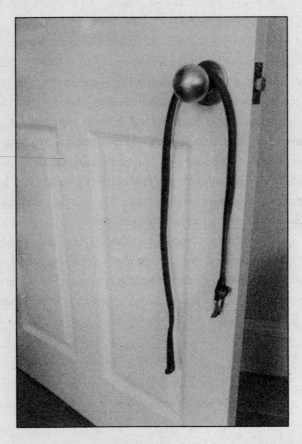

LARRY ITEM #11

I learned many things living with an advertising executive for five years: One of them was that for a company to succeed it needed a marketing niche. It wasn't enough to start up a Web site. I needed a message, a product, something.

Well, a product was out, pretty much because I'm the most unmaterialistic person I know. In fact, I only own seventy-five possessions.

Counting all clothes, underwear, school supplies, recreational equipment, software, key to the family house—seventy-five. It's my little secret; even Beth doesn't know about it.

Most people probably have more than seventy-five things in their top desk drawer, let alone entire life.

My list of guidelines:

If I got a new CD, I either traded for it or had to sell an old one. Same with books and videos (thank God for libraries). I rented skis when I went to the mountains, borrowed basketballs, downloaded free software and music online.

A notebook counts as one, even though it has seventy sheets of paper. A pair of socks counts as one, as do shoes.

I don't keep things like stamps around, don't want to feel tied down by them; I take letters to the post office so the stamps don't even come into my possession.

I've been like this since eighth grade, when I read about some Native Americans not wanting to leave too many "footprints" on the earth when they left. I took it literally. Every single thing I bought was a major, MAJOR decision. I asked myself if I could live up to the responsibility of owning it, maintaining it, housing it. In other words, DO I HAVE TO OWN THIS NEW ITEM SO BADLY THAT IT'S WORTH REMOVING SOMETHING ELSE WITH MEANING FROM MY LIST OF SEVENTY-FIVE SACRED POSSESSIONS?[19]

People always talk about writing what you know. So I got the idea into my head that Larry

_____

[19] This doesn't mean I don't covet certain things; I do. There was a leather jacket I thought of for days, lusted over. Thankfully, the feeling passed when I saw the same jacket on Mr. Perrelli, the assistant principal.

should discuss something he (I) knows about. And anticonsumerism was certainly one of those things. Plus, the topic was just beginning to grab a foothold in the culture; there were all these books coming out about simplifying your life. Kids were crossing out logos on T-shirts. Maybe they were only a few freedom fighters, but I thought it could really be a trend in the making. I liked being at the forefront of a movement. And, with Peter being head of a giant advertising agency, it gave me the feeling of sleeping with the enemy, a *Spy vs. Spy* vibe that excited me.

So it was decided—Larry's mission statement would be to take on waste and overspending and cultural brainwashing.

Unless I felt like writing about something else, of course.

I'm not saying I came up with this elaborate plan to impress Beth during her extended Thoreau phase.

Let's just say it didn't hurt.

The first Larry meeting was held in Mr. Blake's Spanish room after school at two-thirty. The tiny classroom overflowed with kids from every clique—Goths, jocks, wallflowers, techies, shop rats, nerds, even a few cheerleaders. (As if jocks weren't bad enough, we needed people to cheer them on? Please.)

"Everyone!" Beth yelled. "Let's get going."

I made Beth promise to hold the reins herself. Being involved in your own fan club was one thing; running it was something else entirely.

Marlon raised his hand. "My friend in Wichita said there's a sticker in the bathroom of a bookstore on Route 101 that says 'Larry.'"

"My cousin in L.A. said the kids in her school set up a new Larry link that gets over a hundred hits a day," Jessica added.

"My sister went to ski camp and saw a guy wearing a 'Larry for President' button," Eli said.

I tried to close my gaping mouth but couldn't. April Fool's Day was last week, wasn't it?

I was now face-to-face with the downside of living in semi-isolation. Sure, Larry was an up-and-coming site, but stickers and buttons? No one had mentioned them in the chat rooms.

Then I remembered my conversation with Flip-Off a few days ago about changing the world. And the light came on as if after a power failure—I *was* changing the world. A tiny bit at a time, of course, but still. I was out there, I was contributing. Even the undersized desk and chair I sat in couldn't contain me anymore.

Leah from my homeroom talked about Larry's commitment to making the world a better place. Had I ever uttered that sentiment to her on any given morning, the look of disdain on her face would have been enough to jackhammer me into the concrete floor. The meeting ended with Jessica singing a song she had written about Larry's influence on her life. Jessica was this Goth chick who had permanent dibs on the spot outside the gym to smoke between classes. I usually ran from the gaze of her heavily outlined eyes, but today I found myself quite moved. These people, who wouldn't talk to me if I burst into flames in the middle of study hall, were analyzing and interpreting Larry's every word.

"It's so great to focus on the big picture, not just our stupid little lives at school." Beth bounced down the corridor as she spoke to me. "We'll go to my house and brainstorm. You want to stay for dinner?"

Suddenly the evolution of the world's spiritual growth seemed meaningless compared to my relationship with Beth reaching a new level. I tried to remain calm.

"Sounds great."

"Good, it's settled."

As we passed the gym, I heard a grunt that pounded my heart like a stone. Beth unhooked her arm from mine, then wheeled around to face Todd.

"I thought you had practice?" she asked.

"It's canceled. The coach ate some bad fish for lunch."

Speaking of bad fish . . . I stared at his jacket so I wouldn't have to look at his face.

He should have been nicknamed The Wizard instead of me, because Beth's personality and voice changed right before my eyes.

"Oh, no. I hope he's okay."

I shot her a look that bordered on contempt. She elbowed me back—hard.

"My mom's still at work," he told her. "Want to come over?"

Somehow I knew I wasn't included in the invitation.

"I think that's doable," she answered.

I pulled Beth aside. "I thought you were over him," I half-whispered, half-shouted.

"Look, I feel bad about this, I do. But I've got to keep my options open."

And with that, Beth slammed the door on the elaborate fantasy I had already constructed in my feeble mind. Even worse, the idea never occurred to Todd that I might possibly be considered a threat. I was as hazardous to his position as a flea.

I got back in her face. "The big picture— yeah, right."

"What's your problem? Can't we work on this tomorrow?" she asked.

I told her tomorrow I was working on my Frisbee robotics project.

"We'll definitely reschedule." She waved goodbye in front of Todd, who still hadn't noticed my presence.[20]

How can you do this to me? He's boring and I'm, I'm . . . but I knew the word *Larry* would never emerge from my lips. The sad thing was, even Larry couldn't compare to the hormonal tug of Todd Terrific. I looked up toward the heavens, or at least to the stained ceiling tile of the hall.

"Mom. This sucks. Help."

And I stood there until I knew what I needed to do.

Then I ran.

---

[20] If his face were any blanker, you could show movies on it.

I usually wrote my sermons sitting on the swing in my basement, but this called for a whole new level of solitude. I rode my bike past the stores, past the theater, toward the nature preserve behind the cemetery. Until I got my all-terrain, I used to leave my bike at the top of the trail and hike in.[21] Now I bounced over roots and rocks with ease. I'd have only an hour and a half of daylight, but with this much adrenaline pulsing through me that was all the time I'd need.

I pulled my bike up against a cluster of maples and hiked about half a mile. The trail disappeared, and I crawled through the brambles until I reached the familiar birch and woodpile. I brushed the leaves aside, moved the tarp, and descended into the large hole.

---

[21] Possession #54—I had to sell my guitar to get it.

My underground room measured ten by twelve paces, pretty much the size of my bedroom at home. From top to bottom it was seven feet. A few years ago, it had taken me a month of afternoons and Saturdays to dig it. Since then, I came once a week to think or un-think, as the case may be.

I folded my blanket into quarters and sat down on the thawing earth. I took the fully charged laptop from my pack and began.

SERMON #113

Okay—this sermon is off the usual topic, but I've got to write about it anyway.

Can we talk about phonies? About people who pretend they're your best friend—no, they ARE your best friend— until somebody better comes along?

People climbing their way up the social ladder are just as bad as people climbing their way up the corporate one. Moving from one clique to another, checking out the people on the next rung, working their way up like freaking caterpillars until one day—poof!— they leave one rung for good, on to bigger and better things. Then they get rejected in the new clique, of course, and come slithering back to their friends on the lower rung. And you're supposed to sit there like some dope guarding seats at a concert, never realizing your friends found a better section and have left you behind.

Well, I don't know about you, but I am sick and tired of welcoming the same old people back into the fold. Hey, once you make the choice to move on— move on! Don't come back when your new friends leave, don't come back when somebody breaks up with you, don't come back when you want to feel like yourself again 'cause you're tired of spending all that energy trying to act like somebody you're not and you just want to be accepted by people who always liked the real you.

Tired of keeping up the front of being some witty, gorgeous, happy, considerate person you're not? Tired of waiting for your "new" friends to appreciate your inner self? Well, too bad. Take two aspirin and DON'T CALL ME IN THE MORNING.

* * *

Well, THAT felt better. . . . As much as I wanted to, I knew I couldn't send it out right away. Beth would never in a million years suspect that I was Larry, but still, the timing of this one was a tad obvious. I'd save it and e-mail it later, let Beth think she was safe from Larry's gaze for a few brief moments.

I made a list of some upcoming topics: national antishopping day, corporate boycotts, and celebrity worship. I snapped my PC shut and took a few deep breaths. If I sat in this pit for the rest of my life, I could never get enough of the damp earth smell. It was the mixture of life and death that attracted me, nature's primordial scent. I climbed out, covered my hideout, then stood in tree pose among the maples. Almost twilight, my favorite time of day.

As a kid, I was addicted to Game Boys. My fingers punched those buttons day and night; I loved the mental and visual stimulation. It's strange, but the opposite was also true. I loved the silence, the openness of the forest. I felt humbled by its weight, and the thought of uttering anything seemed ridiculously unnecessary. Every time I came here, the same thought returned—live here, keep spreading the word, be a hermit, escape from the crap, from the stuff, from the phonies. Could a culture junkie like me disconnect from civilization and still live? Thoreau did; could I?

I lay back against the tree. Luckily, I didn't have to decide today.

LARRY ITEMS #14 and #32

Two days later, I attended Beth's piano recital—all Bach. Even more than the music, I loved the way she grinned through her mistakes, not nervous like the other musicians, just ecstatic at being able to make music, flaws and all.

On the ride home we complained about the college application process, especially the essays. "You need a crystal ball to answer them," she said. "Everyone says just to make stuff up, but I can't. You know how I feel about being honest."

I slumped back into the seat and changed the subject.

When I saw her the next day, she was at my back door waving a piece of paper. Her cheeks were flushed as if she'd just heard bad news. "Have you read today's sermon?"

I grabbed the paper from her hand. With her concert, I had forgotten all about my rant in the woods. I asked her why it upset her so much.

"It's *me*! It's the other day with Todd. I was so insensitive. And all he wanted to do was fool around anyway."

"You can't possibly be surprised."

"The only thing I'm surprised at is what a glutton for punishment I am . . . such a loser."

She looked me straight in the eye. "Feel free to stop me anytime."

I motioned for her to continue.

"Are you sure you didn't call Larry up and ask him to write this?" she asked. "It's so appropriate, it's scary."

I almost dropped the glass of seltzer in my hand. "Yeah, he said, 'No problem, Josh. I'll get right on it.' "

She asked me if I'd seen Larry's latest possession. "It's a man's watch," she said. "But women wear them all the time. At least my mother does."

"Maybe your mom is Larry."

"Yeah, right. And a statue of some Hindu deity. I looked it up."

"Ganesh. I saw it this morning." I felt a wave of anxiety break inside me. The statue had belonged to my mom; I kept it wrapped in my closet. The only reason I posted it so soon was because Beth had never seen it.

"Then maybe you saw this too." Beth handed me another piece of paper and, thankfully, changed the subject.

The printout also came from the Larry site, copied from one of the bulletin boards.

COME OUT, COME OUT, WHEREVER YOU ARE. LARRY, WHY ARE YOU HIDING BEHIND YOUR ANONYMOUS SCREEN NAME? WHO ARE YOU? AFRAID NO ONE WOULD LISTEN IF WE ALL KNEW WHAT A LOSER YOU WERE?
—betagold

I'd read messages from betagold before— he/she actually wrote/shouted in quite often, but never with this amount of confrontation.

"What does this have to do with us?" I asked.

"Well, hopefully the nutjobs aren't going to start coming out of the woodwork. I mean, can Larry have some peace, do you mind?"

I took a new jar of peanut butter from the cupboard and cut up some apples from the bowl on the table. Betagold's message was certainly disconcerting; the last thing I needed was to blow my cover in front of Beth. I handed her the peanut butter and a spoon. She dipped the spoon into the virgin jar.

"Like being the first person to walk in the snow," she said.

I've always fought to be the first person to nail a new jar of Jif, but it was worth giving that up just to watch Beth lick the spoon clean.

Beth looked at me with her most determined expression. "I give you full permission to go into my father's store . . ."

"Aisle three, on the left."

". . . take down a giant ball peen hammer . . ."

"Rubber handle, better grip."

". . . and bang me on the head repeatedly the next time I jump at any guy's command."

"I'm not sure if Pavlov himself could deprogram you that easily."

It was that simple. We were back to our old selves. We ate apples and peanut butter like we did in grade school and talked about what kind of tattoos our teachers would get if we forced them into it. She told me about her cousin in Seattle having surgery; I told her how worried I was that Katherine might actually move in with Peter and me.

After Beth left for the hardware store, I hurried to the computer to see betagold's message for myself. "AFRAID NO ONE WOULD LISTEN IF WE ALL KNEW WHAT A LOSER YOU WERE?" Was betagold right? Is that one of the reasons why I hid behind my screen name? I typed out a generic response with phrases like "freedom of speech" and "the right to privacy." But deep inside I worried about something much less constitutional.

What if somebody found me out before I reached my desired level of contribution? I had to get moving, step up Larry's productivity. The sermons were fun, but I was already getting tired of my own voice. Let's face it, my sermons were just my opinions, mixed in with a little rhetoric and passion. If some people were moved by them—great. The last thing I wanted to do, however, was lecture other kids. I felt strongly about these things, sure. But hey, make up your own mind. It's not like I'm an expert on anyone but me.

I decided to keep up the sermons but expand the Web site with additional features. Attract some new people, make things a little punchier.

If betagold was planning to out me, he or she had better think again.

How about this for a fashion show?

On one side of the runway, you've got models wearing the trendy clothes kids spend their hard-earned money on. Cruising down the other side, you've got the poverty-stricken youth from Southeast Asia who make this "must-have" collection. The contrast should be enlightening—or maybe just embarrassing.

Doesn't anyone else care about the increasing gap between the haves and the have-nots? Millions of people wearing the finest clothes, eating the best food, driving the fastest cars, while most of the world's population eat a small bowl of food, then sleep on a mat for a few hours, resting up for another eighteen-hour workday.

Did you know that HALF of the SIX BILLION people on the planet live on less than TWO DOLLARS a day? The price of a cup of designer coffee at Starbucks. Makes me sick just thinking about it.

Our STUFF lives better than most of the people in the world do.

To say nothing of how we're treating

nature. Drill for oil in the Arctic Circle? Why not. Rich white men need to get richer, don't they? Drop the emission standards so gas companies can turn a bigger profit? Sure! Why worry about the ozone layer when we've got stockholders to think about?

Nature is going to mutiny one of these days—giant earthquakes or floods just to evict our sorry asses.

I mean, doesn't anyone remember the Lorax? Who is speaking for the trees these days? We're producing and consuming ourselves into oblivion, completely out of touch with the real world, the natural world. If your life depended on it, could you tell what time it was by the sun? Could you find north without a compass? Could you tell the difference between a white oak and a red maple? Didn't think so.

We're not fit to live in the world anymore; we're tourists, clear-cutting our way across the planet till nothing's left.

(In case you're interested, the maple's the one with the wide three-pointed leaves.)

Over the next several weeks, I slowly started noticing that Larry might, just might, be having an effect on the rest of the world. In the next town over, citizens boycotted the new superstore trying to move in. Coincidence? Maybe. Maybe not. The school's baseball team actually went on strike, saying they didn't want to be billboards for Nike anymore because of the workers' conditions. The amazing thing was, most of the students supported them.

At first I thought this was happening at my school because the Larry vortex emanated so close by. But according to several newspaper and magazine articles, students across the country were beginning to reject the commercialism being shoved down their throats. The consumer backlash was bound to happen sooner or later—ebb and flow, supply and demand, that sort of thing. Did Larry deserve a tiny piece of the credit? Who knows?

My feelings of joy were short-lived, though, because betagold left another message on the bulletin board.

I JUST WANT YOU TO KNOW I'M CLOSING IN ON YOU, LARRY. AND IT'S NOT FROM ANALYZING YOUR POSSESSIONS EITHER. I'M GOING TO TRACK YOU DOWN MY WAY. YOU MUST BE USING A CELL PHONE, THAT'S WHY I CAN'T TRACE YOUR MODEM LINE. BUT SOONER OR LATER, I'LL TRACK THAT DOWN TOO. I KNOW SOMEONE AT THE PHONE COMPANY, AND THEY'RE COMING UP WITH NEW TRACKING SYSTEMS ALL THE TIME. LOTS OF PEOPLE THINK YOU'RE DOING GOOD WORK, BUT I THINK SOMEONE WHO DOESN'T STAND BEHIND HIS/HER WORDS IS A COWARD. EVEN THE NEWSPAPERS PRINT THE NAMES OF PEOPLE WHO WRITE INTO THE EDI-TORIALS.

P.S. IT'S NOT THAT I DISAGREE WITH WHAT YOU'RE SAYING—I HATE CONSUMERISM TOO. I JUST THINK THE WORLD DESERVES TO KNOW WHO YOU ARE.

P.P.S. DO YOU LIVE IN NEW ENGLAND, LARRY? HOME OF THOREAU AND EMERSON, YOUR IDOLS? LOTS OF RED MAPLES UP THERE.

The pen that had been clenched between my teeth fell into my lap. I was usually meticulous about not putting anything in the sermons that could lead to me, but red maples—who would have thought? And who was betagold anyway—a botanist detective? There was no way he or she could track me down, especially not based on a tree. I had a plan, goals. What did betagold think—this was some kind of game? I made a note to get a new cell phone line, then I put my pen back between my teeth and typed a response:

AS I TOLD YOU BEFORE, I FEEL MY IDENTITY ONLY GETS IN THE WAY OF MY WORK. IF I TELL PEOPLE WHO COME TO THIS SITE THAT I'M BLACK OR A COLLEGE PROFESSOR OR A RETIRED BUSINESSWOMAN, SUDDENLY EVERY-THING I SAY GETS FILTERED THROUGH THAT. SOME PEOPLE MIGHT CHOOSE NOT TO HEAR THE THOUGHTS OF SOMEONE FROM A CERTAIN DEMOGRAPHIC. HOW ABOUT CONCENTRATING ON WHAT I HAVE TO SAY INSTEAD OF THE MEASLY IDENTITY OF THE WRITER?

P.S. I'VE NEVER BEEN TO NEW ENGLAND. IS IT NICE?

I wasn't happy about having to lie in the postscript, but I didn't have much choice. If betagold was on a mission and was anything like me, this harassment wouldn't stop until Larry was uncovered.

And the worst of it was, just like me, betagold could be anyone. Somebody I already knew.

Anyone at all.

My mother always understood how curious my mind could get and put in many hours trying to keep it busy.[22] But with her gone, my insatiable hunger for knowledge sometimes crept into the mischievous category—witness my online interlude with poor Ms. Phillips or the time I broke into the high school on a Saturday night and set all the clocks back fifteen minutes just to mess up the routine. So when I picked the lock on Peter's briefcase one night at two a.m., it was pretty much just business as usual.

The internal memos seemed innocuous enough—demographic surveys and reports from many of Peter's top advertising clients. As I skimmed through them, however, it became clear that

---

[22] Like drawing blueprints of the local bank so I could pretend to rob it, that kind of thing.

they were extremely confidential[23]—future ad
campaigns, most aimed at the "lucrative youth
market."[24] I checked out the ads. Joe Camel was
gone, but the tobacco companies weren't giving
up on the illegal teen market. An ad for a
major designer deflected the criticism of paying Asian workers only dollars a day.[25] A beer
company wanted to come up with a print ad as
collectible as the vodka ads traded by teenagers. It went on and on, enough material to
hang corporate America by its designer tie.

I scanned the report onto my hard drive, then
put the original back in Peter's briefcase.

I was furious with Peter's involvement in
all this. Hey, thanks for the roof over my
head, the food in the cupboards, but do young
women in Indonesia have to suffer for my well
being? Not in the world I want to live in.

I sat up all night creating my own ads. I
made the Gap model look more anorexic than she
was, I turned the swoosh into a swastika, I

---

[23] Just the word *classified* stamped across the pages raised
my blood pressure by at least 25 points.

[24] Teens spent more than $141 BILLION last year on stuff; did
you know that?

[25] They still wanted to pay them a few dollars, they just
didn't want people to hate them for it.

even hooked the men in the cigarette ads up to oxygen machines. I hadn't had this much fun since I hacked my way into Blockbuster's system and ordered a hundred copies of *Pee-Wee's Big Adventure*.[26]

I didn't worry about Peter. If he had this information, other bigwig executives did too. I posted my new ads onto Larry's Web site, hoping for some kind of reaction.

Two hundred sixty-seven people responded by breakfast. Kids posted ads of their own; some of them created parodies of the companies in my ads, some came up with new ones.[27]

The ads actually made me feel closer to Peter; I was following in his footsteps in a subversive, anticonsumer way. I enjoyed commenting on the world of advertising without being in it.

And for a perennial outsider like me, that was a giant plus.

---

[26] Three copies were definitely not enough.

[27] My favorite was a Tommy Hilfiger ad with several black men at a boathouse. Underneath it someone wrote, "How can we afford to go yachting when there are no jobs here because you make everything overseas?"

LARRY ITEMS #26, #2, #17, #21

"It's official! He's a guy!" Beth said.

"Unless he's a plus size woman who wears boxers."

She pelted me again.[28]

I rubbed my arm and asked her if we should track Larry down.

"Absolutely not. Suppose he's some geek with a mullet, living in the Everglades? I don't want to know!"

Reason #56 not to tell her.

If Beth had read betagold's message the other day, she didn't mention it now.

"I've been doing research on consumerism since last fall," she said. "And I've never seen any of that information he just posted. Either Larry has great sources or he's starting to make stuff up."

---

[28] I'd take all the physical contact I could get.

"Are you kidding? Corporate America? There's miles of stuff we don't know."

"You're right. Of course, you're right."

We sat in the cafeteria with a deck of tarot cards Beth's twenty-two-year-old sister, Marie, had given her. Beth kept looking at the instructions as she turned the cards over, her face growing more serious by the minute. She suddenly swept all the cards off the table and shoved them in her bag.

"What's the matter?" I asked.

"Nothing." She shifted her eyes away from me. "These cards are stupid. You can't read someone's fortune. I don't even know why Marie gave them to me. More mumbo-jumbo crap we don't need."

"It was bad, right? I can take it."

She took the cards out and showed me the one on top—a skeleton rowing a boat out to sea. "Death, okay? See how lame they are? As if you're going to die."

I stared at the skeleton and couldn't help shivering. "Maybe this came up because I'm going to the cemetery today."

She almost jumped from her chair in relief. "Yes, of course! Three years ago, right? I knew it was this week."

She rummaged through her science notebook and pulled out a cream-colored envelope with "Mrs. Swensen" written on the front. "Can you put this with the flowers? It's just a little note, like last year."

Good old Beth. I wanted to tell her she was the only person who truly comforted me when my mother died. But from my emotional straitjacket, all I said instead was "Thanks." I shuffled off to my next class with my heart aching.

I knew it was wrong, but during biology lab I stuck the tip of my pen under the envelope flap and opened Beth's letter. "Dear Mrs. Swensen, I still miss you, we all do. Josh is doing great; you'd be proud. Keep watching over us. Love, Beth." Not too sappy, just the right amount of sentiment. Beth had always been Mom's favorite.

I stopped at the florist on the way home from school and got a big bouquet of tulips for my mother's grave. ("Two lips are better than one," Mom used to say.) Peter pulled up to the house, preoccupied and harried, doing what he always did this time of year—throwing himself into his work. We drove most of the way in awkward silence.

"Katherine wanted to come today," Peter finally said. He waited for my reaction, but I didn't give him one. "I thought it might be too soon," he added.

The thought of making this pilgrimage with the odds-on favorite for my new stepmother made me cringe. "Well, that was nice she wanted to come," I said, completely for his benefit.

"Do you think so? I thought so too." It was one of those only-child moments when your parent forgets you are his kid and just talks to you like a regular person. We had been having more of these moments lately; I liked them.

Peter swung the Jeep into the lane near Mom's grave and we both got out. Soon the rose bushes lining the path would be in full bloom. I could find my way to the spot blindfolded—twenty-two headstones from the corner, sixteen in.

"They just put the monument back last week," Peter said. "Stupid vandals spray-painted this whole row."

Sure enough, the two stones next to Mom's were covered with red squiggly lines.

"They had a heck of a time cleaning the granite," Peter continued. "But it looks like they did a pretty good job."

I nodded. The back of her tombstone showed only the faintest traces of paint. But graffiti would have been a welcome relief compared to what awaited me on the other side of the stone. There, etched into the granite underneath Mom's name and dates, were my own.

JOSHUA SWENSEN
1983-

I stared at Peter, too stunned for words.

"While they had the stone out to be cleaned, it only made sense to put your name on too. The guy at the monument place said it was definitely the smart thing to do."

"Probably 'cause it's not his name," I answered.

"Your mother thought you'd want to be buried here. I told her you might want a plot of your own with your family someday, but she said you came into the world with her, might as well go out too."

"I *do* want to be buried here," I said. "Just not now. Having my name on the stone is kind of sick, don't you think?"

He ran his finger across the letters. "It does take some getting used to. Seems so permanent this way."

A shrill noise filled the afternoon sky. I knew it was one of the crows in the birch nearby, but the picture on Beth's tarot card flashed into my mind, as if the skeleton itself was cawing, laughing as he rowed into the darkness.

JOSHUA SWENSEN JOSHUA SWENSEN JOSHUA SWENSEN

The first number was 1983, but what would the second number be? I stood in front of the tombstone as if it held the answer—like a wide-eyed tourist standing around a roulette table in Las Vegas, waiting to see where the spinning ball would land: 2061? 2043? Or maybe something sooner, like 2002? The purpose of this depressing visit was to reflect on my mother's death. Little did I know I'd be pondering my own.

I took some photographs, then laid the tulips on the grass, placing the envelope from Beth behind them. We both said a few silent prayers, then Peter moved several steps back, the way he always did, to give me some time alone with Mom.[29] I stood silently and prayed, but if truth be told, I still felt her spirit much closer in the makeup department at Bloomingdale's.

---

[29] As if we both knew she always belonged more fully to me than to him. (I guess not joining us in the burial plot was his way of releasing us back to the universe without him.)

On the drive back, my mind ping-ponged between the skeleton in the boat and my name carved into the headstone. I was only seventeen and in perfectly good health; dying seemed ludicrous. However, I had always been superstitious. Maybe these signs pointed to another part of me dying—namely Larry. Maybe betagold was gaining on me, and Larry didn't have long to live.

As Peter and I drove home in silence, my mind raced. It was too soon to give Larry up. His work wasn't finished.

Yet.

Let's talk today about consuming something a little different, shall we?

How about the feast of celebrities
we all dine on?

What are they up to? Who's getting
divorced? Who's got the eating disorder? Who's cheating on a spouse?

Eat it up—first by the spoonfuls,
then by the wheelbarrows, then by giant
Mack trucks filled with gossip and tid-
bits and CRAP about other people's
lives.

Why are you concerned with people
who don't care one iota about your life?
Maybe because you don't have one . . .

And while you're at it, make sure
those televisions are going all the
time—round-the-clock sitcoms and "info-
tainment."

Eat! Stuff yourself! There's always
more. Step right up—your fifteen minutes of fame have arrived! Let us worship YOU! Talk into the microphone,
look into the camera—we want to know
EVERYTHING about you.

And after we've picked your bones clean, we'll move on to the next victim.

See those skeletons over there? They are all that remain of the celebrities you used to worship. That one on top? He was in one of those boy-bands you tore your hair out over last year.

Such a shame.

Such a waste.

He was such a lovely boy.

Who knows why some things take off? Pet Rocks, Crazy Bones, Hula-Hoops? *Who Wants to Be a Millionaire?* Sometimes the culture just grabs on to something and pulls. And pulls and pulls and pulls. It makes no sense; there's no reason for it. If there had been warning signs, maybe I would have noticed.

As Larry continued to post each of his possessions, word of mouth increased. He's a guy, he wears jeans, he can't be too old. Or can he be? The chat rooms overflowed with theories. Soon, a cult developed that analyzed each item, building a profile of who Larry might be. I spent as much time planning which item to post as I did on my sermons. Larry's total hits grew by more than 90 percent each day.

As the school year came to an end, graduation and prom became the only topics of conversation. Since I wasn't attending either, May should have gone along at a nice, manageable clip. If two things—utterly beyond my control—hadn't happened.

The first cosmic tweak came from a college freshman named Billy North, at the University of Georgia. According to his Web site, Billy loved to play solitaire, fly remote-controlled airplanes, and surf the Internet. I guess he also liked to manipulate words and letters the way I used to play with the magnetic numbers on my mom's fridge. Well, he must have had a chunk of free time on his hands, because he printed out all of Larry's sermons. Then he printed out Larry's logo, got a pair of scissors, and cut four small rectangles, removing the plug, floppy disk, dove, and planet from inside the peace sign. He took this Larry "stencil" and placed it over each of the sermons. Sure enough, a pattern of words emerged: east, city, water, boy. Billy posted this series of words on Larry's bulletin board, and suddenly identifying Larry from the hidden clues became all the rage. Kids logged on to analyze the latest sermons with a fervor that hadn't been seen since people scoured the cover of *Abbey Road* for clues of Paul's death.

I tried not to laugh when I read his original message, but when I placed the peace stencil over the sermons myself, I had to admit his theory held some water. Many of the words did point to me. I used one of my other screen names to post this message:

> IF LARRY KNOWS ABOUT YOUR WHOLE SYSTEM, THEN IT'S NO GOOD ANYMORE, RIGHT? HE'LL JUST PUT WORDS IN THE WINDOWS THAT LEAD YOU AWAY FROM HIM. —24ME

Billy posted this back:

> IT'S A SUBCONSCIOUS THING. LARRY WANTS TO BE FOUND OUT. HE'LL END UP GIVING HIM-SELF AWAY. HE CAN'T SUBVERT MY SYSTEM.

Needless to say, I now spent much more time editing my sermons. Instead of just concentrating on the words, I had the architecture of the piece to think about.[30] And Billy North was right about one thing; no matter how I tried, the words in the stencil's window very often described me—young, quirky, reader. I had to fight myself to change them. I hated to admit it but a few times I actually left them in. Maybe Billy was right and Larry would sabotage his career.

---

[30] If truth be told, it was a challenge I took to immediately.

Of course, it was only a matter of time before betagold chimed in with an opinion:

LARRY, YOU CAN'T POSSIBLY THINK I NEED THIS COCKAMAMIE PRAYER WHEEL—OR THOSE PHOTOGRAPHS—TO FIND YOU. I'M GOING TO TRACK YOU DOWN THE OLD-FASHIONED WAY, WITH PURE DETERMINATION. ALL THE CRACK-POTS MIGHT BE HAVING FUN WITH WORDS, BUT REST ASSURED THIS IS NO GAME TO ME.—betagold

Between Billy and his wacked-out theory and betagold's Lt. Gerard mission, I should've quit while I was ahead. There were a dozen reasons to stop, and the rational part of me knew every one verbatim. But the part of me that loved to race down the highway in my car seat, the part whose adrenal glands surged with those fight-or-flight hormones, that part wanted to keep Larry going. Not only wanted to continue but wanted to risk it all and go for broke. As I twirled around in my hammock swing, I knew a boatload of reasons wouldn't make me stop being Larry. He was the perfect alter ego for a loner like me—outspoken and opinionated. He didn't need to bury himself in a privacy cocoon, like good old Josh.

The risk was its own reward. So I started working on pseudo ads skewering Benetton and Abercrombie & Fitch. There still was a lot to be done to fight the tsunami of consumerism, and I was sure as hell going to do my share.

You want me, betagold? Come and get me.

LARRY ITEMS #33, #42, #50, #51, #73

The next thing that happened made the whole Billy North thing seem almost normal.

One of Larry's sermons — the one about the richest nations consuming themselves into oblivion while almost half of the *six billion* people on the planet live on less than *two dollars a day*[31] — had stirred up many discussions in the chat rooms. Larry wrote a follow-up about the World Bank and how it could help Third World countries by forgiving them some of their debt.[32] The sermon had been posted weeks ago with not a lot of fanfare.

Until Bono read it.

It seems that U2's lead singer was doing

---

[31] I'm writing it again because it's important.

[32] Why should the poorest nations have to pay back the richest nations, especially when the loans had been taken out by dictators long gone? It was one of Larry's "preachier" sermons, but my personal favorite.

research for a presentation he was giving to the U.S. Senate on his pet topic—the World Bank and Third World debt—when he turned up Larry's sermon. The sermon intrigued him; he checked out the site and loved the anticonsumer, free-the-people-from-corporate-oppression spirit. This would have been all well and good if U2 hadn't also released a new song. The subject was antimaterialism and it *rocked.* Bono had written it months before, and it had absolutely nothing to do with my sermons, but a few fervent Larry fans didn't care. They adopted the song as their own.

The new song led to a video—a wild smorgasbord with so much STUFF in it that if you weren't a believer in cutting back consumption before you watched it you sure as hell were after.

Of course, the video led to interviews and articles.

Then a tour.

And over the next several weeks, all these wonderful, amazing things led U2's millions and millions of fans to one place.

Larry's Web site.

Now, I'm not saying I wasn't flattered—OF COURSE I WAS. I had grown up on their music; my mother had been their biggest fan.[33] But as much as I was insanely ecstatic that Bono was talking to Kurt Loder about Larry, I also knew that one of the key tenets of Larry's philosophy was against celebrity worship. I was torn. I would have cut off my right arm with a Weedwacker to meet Bono. On the other hand,[34] I knew I should lead my own life and let Bono live his. It was a confusing yet thrilling time.

"I logged onto Larry this morning," Beth said when she dropped by for breakfast. "There were already over a million hits."

"What?" I raced downstairs, then realized Beth was right behind me. I did a mental scan of the stuff on my desk and determined it was safe.

"A million point three," I said watching the counter click off hits as we spoke. "I hope Larry's got enough memory."

"That's a weird thing to worry about." Beth looked at me with the suspicious look she usually saved for guys trying to pick her up.

---

[33] In one of the last photos I have of her, her hair is almost gone and she's lying on the couch wearing her *Joshua Tree* T-shirt. I had been named for the tall, twisted evergreen after my pregnant mother had visited a friend in Arizona. When the U2 album came out four years later, she memorized every song.

[34] Using this example, that would be my left.

I told her I just didn't want Larry's site to crash.

"I'm worried about more than that. I'm worried that Larry's message will get diluted in all this, this—"

"Commercialism." I finished the sentence for her.

"It's good news, of course. I mean, we're talking about Bono here, Amnesty International, the whole thing. I just hope it doesn't get out of control." She looked me over again. "You okay?"

I told her I was, and said I'd meet her at the hardware store later.

After she left, I watched the Web site's counter continue to click, a veritable McDonald's of hungry spiritual searchers. I looked up to the beamed ceiling and prayed.

"Mom?"

I tried again. "Mom? This is good, yes? Getting the message out to more people?"

The house remained silent.

"I shouldn't worry, right, Mom?"

The next sound I heard was laughter—loud, guttural guffaws coming from the kitchen where Katherine and Peter had just entered the house. It must have been one hell of a joke Peter told, because Katherine didn't stop.

"Mom, this isn't funny," I said.

But the universe didn't care; it just continued to fill the house with enough laughter
to send a pack of hyenas running for cover.

Which is what I should have done.

I decided to stop being paranoid and work with what the universe had presented me.[35]

Even though it was the last week of school, the club's membership had swelled to include more than 78 percent of the senior class.[36] Beth clapped her hands and the meeting came to order.

"Okay. U2 has turned millions of people on to Larry. The question is: How do we ensure Larry's message doesn't get lost in all the brouhaha?"

That's my girl—getting to the crux of the matter immediately. Her question mirrored my own concerns, which had kept me up several nights that week. I'd even gone so far as to stay up eating handfuls of M&M's and playing Peter's mancala game. My insomnia became so

---

[35] The half-empty school of thought did nothing for me.

[36] Including a few teachers, which was weird.

frenzied, however, that I ended up tossing a couple of glass stones into my mouth instead of M&M's, almost leading to a full-blown dental crisis.

I tried to keep a low profile at these meetings. Luckily, many other kids were involved. Sharon showed us a group of stickers she'd designed.

The first one read, NO MORE STUFF.

Good, right to the point.

Sharon flashed the next layout. STOP SELLING US CRAP.

That one met with hoots and applause.

"These are a series," Sharon said, "to plaster on print ads, billboards, whatever." She held them up.

THIS AD INSULTS ME.

THIS AD INSULTS KIDS.

THIS AD INSULTS WOMEN.

"And my personal favorite, WHOEVER DIES WITH THE MOST STUFF IS STILL COMPLETELY, DE FACTO DEAD."

Barry discussed the pseudo ads he was copying onto posters. When everybody kicked in, we had enough money to print several hundred. We designated the next Saturday as "antistuff" day—a day when we would plaster the city with anticommercialist propaganda. It was my job to post our idea on Larry's Web site in case any other groups across the country wanted in.[37]

After the meeting Beth and I walked home together.

"We'll hit the mall first," she said, "then as many superstores as we can."

I asked her if I should borrow Peter's car.

"No, let's take our bikes. If we're going to be activists, let's go all the way."

"Put the active back in activism," I said.

"Why didn't you say that at the meeting? That would have made a great poster."

She then proceeded to throw me a giant curve ball. "You're not going, are you?" she asked.

"Where? To the mall? What are you talking about?"

She swung her arms by her side. "No, to the prom next week."

"Of course not." We walked in silence. "Are you?"

"Someone told me Todd was going to ask me, but I would have said no. Proms are so fake," she said.

"Gruesome," I added. "Not that either of us would know."

---

[37] My first instinct was to draw attention away from myself by acting like it was no big deal.

96

Her smile was so off-kilter, so vulnerable, that I burst out laughing. She did too.

"Two outsiders completely skeeved at the thought of being 'in'—even for just one night." I said it to ease the awkwardness, but deep down I knew both of us would kill to be able to walk in that world if we wanted to. Beth's entrance to that place of parties and home-comings had only happened with the guys she occasionally dated; mine, through Larry. I guess all along our truest connection came from feeling disconnected.

When I got home and checked the Web site, I realized lots of other kids must have been feeling oppressed by advertising too, because the number of pseudo ads continued to increase. Some of the concepts were unbelievably creative.[38]

People from around the world were swapping ideas, making plans to plaster their towns with the various messages. U2 had not hurt Larry's site by spreading the word. The group had empowered it. It was anti-apathy at its best. I upgraded my server, with pleasure.

---

[38] This led me to a cerebral Möbius strip—suppose these same graphic design skills eventually landed these kids high-paying jobs in the corporations they were now bashing? I swung around in my swing, ruminating on that one for a while.

Unfortunately, I had left my handouts near the coffee machine on my way into the house. The horrendous noise I heard in the background was the sound of my stepfather hitting the roof.

He laid out the pseudo ads on the counter as if he were retiling it. "Where did you get these?"

I told him the Larry site.

He pointed to the vodka parody. "Do you know how many people worked on this account? Doing research, design, printing, marketing? Hundreds of people putting dinner on the table because of this ad."

"Probably not as many people as the alcoholic population," I said. "Now *there's* a big group." I waited for him to mention my real father, who died of alcohol poisoning before I was born.[39] Thankfully he didn't.

I tried to listen to his opinion, rein in my growing anger.

He pointed to another ad. "And this one. Easy for some kid on the Internet to complain about starving children in Africa when he's working on a high-end iMac."

---

[39] I wondered sometimes what my dad was like, if I looked like him, but it was like studying the gladiators in ancient Rome; it had nothing whatsoever to do with me.

"He's not," I said.

"Oh? And how do you know?"

"He posted a photo of his laptop," I stammered. "It wasn't an Apple."

"Well, maybe he should start bashing Apple now. Microsoft too. Wait until this Larry guy gets exposed for the nobody he is, then we'll see what all the fuss is about."

"He won't get exposed."

Peter smirked. "Katherine's been doing a lot of research on him. She says it's a matter of time." He gathered the papers off the counter as if they were a bad hand he'd been dealt at cards. "And I don't want to see any more of this crap in my house unless it's in the trash."

I couldn't understand why he was angry. "Why are you so threatened by this?"

It was the wrong thing to ask.

The next thing I knew, an alien must have inhabited my cool and calm stepfather, because he shoved me against the refrigerator.

"No more of this nonsense, you understand? You don't want to go to graduation, I said okay. But this? I won't stand for it!"

I made sure my voice was completely calm before I spoke. "Let go of me."

It was almost as if Peter's spirit flew back into his body. "I . . . I'm sorry." He straightened his tie. "That was completely uncalled-for."

My face darkened with the memory of prying into his briefcase. "No, it's okay."

"These ads . . . they're everywhere. We have to develop all new campaigns. We're under a lot of pressure—the printers, the execs, the salespeople. No one knows where this guy's getting his data."

I hadn't planned on screwing Peter in this scheme; I was just trying to get the information out.[40] I looked at him blankly, wishing for something appropriate to say. He left in silence, the door reverberating behind him.

The inevitable schism between us became achingly obvious. In a few months I would be at Princeton, eventually seeing him just a few times a year.

He was probably as happy about that prospect as I was.

---

[40] Riding the risk buzz—shame on me.

LARRY ITEM #41

"This is a great way to spend a birthday." Beth pedaled no-hands through the back parking lot of the mall.

"Unless we end up in jail," I said.

"Come on, Henry David. Where's your sense of civil disobedience?"

I had one, but it was just a bit worried about getting tossed in the can on some kind of nuisance violation. It wasn't the jail part that concerned me; I didn't want any undue attention focused my way, considering the secret life I was harboring. To say nothing of Peter's wrath.

"So, it looks like Larry lives somewhere cold. New Hampshire, Wisconsin, and Montana have the most votes in the bulletin boards."

"He could live in Florida and still have those boots."

"Not with a total of seventy-five posses-sions."

I told her in that case I voted Wisconsin. Thankfully, it was almost summer, and I didn't have to wear them now.

We locked our bikes, and I couldn't wait any longer. I handed Beth a box. "Happy Birthday."

"You didn't have to," she said.

"Only homemade things, usual rules."

She opened the box carefully and smiled when she saw the necklace.

"I found this old Chinese abacus," I said. "Took it apart and strung the beads on a silk cord. I placed the beads in order so they actually made sense—2,368,586 divided by 682 equals 3,473. That crystal in the middle is the equal sign . . ." I hoped a car would plow into me so I would stop babbling.

"This is amazing. Makes last year's bouill-abaisse mobile seem like no work at all."[41] She slipped on the necklace and fingered the blue stones. "I gave myself a birthday present this year. I've been wanting to show you for days."

To my amazement, she rolled up her pants leg. Above her right ankle was a fresh tattoo

---

[41] Lobster claws, sea glass, scallop shells were all strung on fishing line. It still hung in the window of her bedroom. How had she not gotten the hint?

of a dollar sign in a circle with a slash through it.

"Are you kidding? Do your parents know?"

She shook her head. "I had Marie's ID with me, but the guy didn't even ask for it."

I ran my hand across Beth's skin.[42] "He did a good job."

"I was going to get 'Larry,' but I didn't want to look like a groupie. This kind of said it all."

The thought of Beth sporting a tattoo of my alter ego almost sent me into hyperventilation. I followed her inside the mall like a puppy.

We plastered the halls and rest rooms of the entire mall, easily avoiding the few security guards. Judging by the people who gathered around to read the posters, we even sparked some conversations.

Next we hit Pottery Barn, Virgin Records, the Gap, Nike Town, and Restoration Hardware.[43] We were taking a short break when we saw Mr. Lynch, our biology teacher, approach us. Beth shoved the rest of the posters into her bag.

"We're screwed," I said.

---

[42] Any excuse.

[43] "This is NOT a hardware store," Beth repeated like a mantra.

He sat down at the table. "You're doing a good job," he said. "We Americans are using way more than our share of resources."

Beth and I returned his smile and handed him some of our posters.

"You know what drives me insane?" he continued. "The tiny stickers they put on fruit—it's for the store's convenience, not the customer's. By the time you peel it off, your gorgeous pear is ruined. And you know why they do it? Because no one complains."

In all the time I'd known Mr. Lynch, I'd never seen him so animated. He told us he'd see us next week and moved on.

Beth tossed her bottle of water into the recycling bin and watched Mr. Lynch walk away. "You don't think . . ."

"What?"

"Mr. Lynch?"

"What about him?"

"You know, that he's Larry."

"You're kidding me, right?"

"He wears jeans; he's got boots . . ."

"I'll bet he's even got a watch and a belt," I said. "I thought you didn't want to know."

"It's hard not to be into it, now that everyone else is." She shuddered. "Did I just say that? Shoot me."

We pedaled home with the satisfaction of a job well done.

"I feel like one of those women who worked in the factories when all the men were at war. Really contributing," she said.

"To blowing up the Japanese," I responded.

"And ending the war."

"And almost a civilization."

"You never quit." She smiled and I took it as a compliment.

We sat on her front steps until it was time for her piano lesson.

"Aren't you leaving today?" she asked.

Since there were only a few days left, Peter let me blow off school. The Larry club meetings and mall visits were *way* more social activity than I was comfortable with, and a nature excursion was definitely in order.

"I like my privacy too," Beth said. "But three days alone in the woods . . . you're insane."

"I'll be insane if I *don't* go," I said. "It's not just the privacy—"

"It's the solitude." She'd heard the drill many times before.

I gathered up my things.

"Good job today. Larry would've been proud," she said.

"He'd love that tattoo."

"Think so?"

"I think it's safe to say he'd hold your foot in his hand and kiss every inch of it."

She swatted me. "See you on Wednesday."

I pedaled home, sorry to be leaving Beth for three days but happy to be lying under the stars alone.

Little did I know what could happen in three days.

Ever tried to jump off the consumer carousel and spend some time alone? Not just alone but alone in Nature—no commercials, no visual distractions but the birds and trees. I've been dipping into my Thoreau again—"For every walk is a sort of crusade." That's me, walking in the woods for hours, crusading for the cause, peeling back the layers of STUFF, and letting only the silence seep in.

Nothing to buy out here, nothing to sell. Nothing to throw away, nothing to think about.

In my seclusion, my "real" life seems self-indulgent and superficial. Gossip, chatter, role-playing—our daily lives are the longest-running play in off-Broadway history. We just don't know it.

Is it a waste of time to watch a starling for an hour? To lie on a bed of moss and gaze at the stars? My man Thoreau also said, "He who sits still in a house all the time may be the greatest vagrant of all."

We are meant to be alone in Nature. The word lonely *never comes up.*

PART THREE

"And there came a voice from heaven,
saying, Thou art my beloved Son in
whom I am well pleased."

St. Mark 1:11

Do you know what it's like to be driving along in second gear and then to accidentally pop the shift into fifth? I was expecting to spend lunch with Beth, hear about how she loved the Thoreau sermon,[44] but she yanked me into an alternative reality with her news.

"You will never guess what Bono's doing." We talked about the mega-rock star now as if he were someone we knew personally. "A giant rock festival—U2 is playing!—along with dozens of other bands in a big empty field in Maine. Music, arts and crafts . . ." she read from the paper in her hand, "a spontaneous gathering of anticonsumerism and general goodwill called Larryfest."

---

[44] I was actually nervous; Larry wrote about Nature and Thoreau while I was off in the woods doing the same. The timing was a bit risky, even for me. There were enough Josh/Larry clues for someone like Beth to make the connection, which of course made it all the more exciting.

"LARRYFEST?" I shouted. Was this for real?

"Tens of thousands of people have already signed up," she said. "And believe it or not, Mom told me I could go, since Marie and two of her friends are going. They can give us a ride. We can camp. What do you say?"

"I go away for three days and there's a *festival* in the works?"

"It's our Woodstock," she said.

"Woodstock was in August."

"Well, this one's Fourth of July! Ease up!"

She told me that all the bands were playing for free, and all the companies would sell food and drinks at cost, not just because of the Woodstock '99 debacle but because of Larry's noncommercial agenda. "It's a festival with no crap, no junk, just music and dancing and singing and friendship and ideas. It's going to rock!"

Too stunned for words, I excused myself and headed to the library to log on. Sure enough, the people who had put this together had done it all secretly, as a surprise to Larry. "It's a new culture—for you, for all of us," the e-mail exclaimed in twenty-point purple font. "Larry, whoever you are, stay incognito, but please come!"

I laughed so loudly, Ms. Costanzo, the

librarian, slumped across the room to shush me. The room seemed bare and empty, ready for summer vacation. I turned back to the screen.

I signed up right then and there—Josh Swensen would attend.

I caught up with Beth outside her locker.

"It's incredible," I said. "Of course we're going."

"Todd wanted to catch a ride with us too, but he's got some family thing he can't get out of."

"Todd? I thought he was out of the picture." GEEZ, WHAT ELSE HAPPENED WHILE I WAS GONE?

"He *is* out of the picture; he just needed a ride. Stop wigging."

I suddenly felt overwhelmed with information. After school, I aimed my bike at Bloomingdale's and pedaled like a maniac.

Unfortunately, Marlene wasn't on—some woman with bright pink lipstick and a mole with a three-inch hair waved me away. But Brunhilda herself had no power over me—I plopped down on the padded stool anyway.

"Mom? Can you hear me?" I waited until I felt her presence.

"I'm doing it, Mom. I'm changing the world. Hundreds of thousands of people coming together in peace. It's working, Mom. I'm contributing."

I pictured her in my mind laughing, stuffing envelopes for her latest cause, still wearing the feather earrings she'd worn in college. "I'm so proud of you, Joshie," she would say.

"Will there be anything else?" the Mole Woman asked.

"Yes. Could you please leave me alone for a few more minutes? You're interrupting an almost perfect moment."

She stormed away, and I listened for the next person to walk by with a message from my mother.

"Keep it up," a man told his wife. "It's your life's work."

I raised my fists into the air in victory. I'd always been aware of it before, but now I had to exemplify Larry's beliefs 24/7.

And Larryfest would be the perfect place to start.

But Larry's e-mail from betagold the next day jolted me out of my peace, love, and understanding reverie.

> ARE YOU GOING TO LARRYFEST, LARRY? WITH YOUR JEANS AND YOUR BOOTS? IT SHOULD BE CALLED COWARDFEST OR HIDE-BEHIND-YOUR-SCREEN-NAME-FEST, DON'T YOU THINK? MAYBE WE CAN PLAY A GIANT GAME OF TRUTH OR DARE AND OUT LARRY? BETTER YET, INSTEAD OF A METAL DETECTOR AT THE GATE, HOW ABOUT A POLYGRAPH TEST? OLLIE, OLLIE, OXEN FREE. COME OUT, COME OUT, WHEREVER YOU ARE.
> I WILL BE THERE, LARRY.
> I WILL FIND YOU.
> —betagold

This time, I didn't even respond. Didn't want to give betagold any more ammunition.

Because of betagold and Billy North, I already analyzed Larry's sermons a thousand times before I sent them out, petrified I'd make some innocuous comment about street signs or great blue herons that could lead anyone to me.

Things were going great—school was done, Beth and I started full time at the hardware store, and the pomp and circumcision of graduation was finally over. There was no way betagold could track me down in Maine—there were already 230,000 people signed up; I would be just another face in the crowd, another teen searching for life's deeper meaning.

Either that or I was being set up.

LARRY ITEM #57

Can it be done?

Hundreds of thousands of people coming together to celebrate being free of corporate advertising and greed? Rejoicing in not being consumer puppets, spending our hard-earned money on stuff we don't need just so a few fat cats can get rich?

Can we do it without violence, without anger?

Can girls and women feel safe and respected?

Can we do it without product endorsements?

Can differences of opinion be tolerated, even celebrated?

I don't know.

I guess we'll find out.

See you there.

Love,

Larry

P.S. I'll be the guy with the T-shirt and the smile.

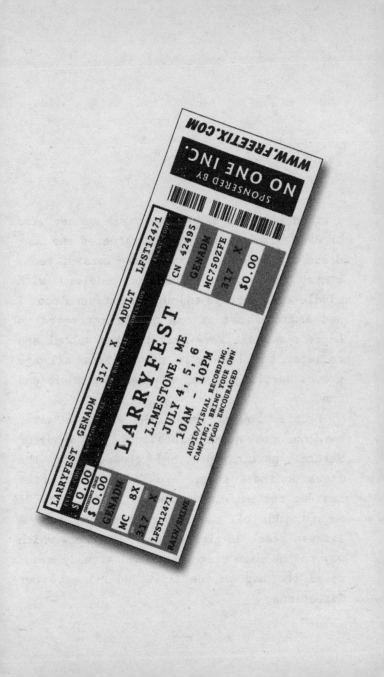

I stood in front of the Larryfest banner, too shocked to move. Larry's logo greeted the hundreds of thousands of visitors—lots of teenagers, but to my amazement toddlers with middle-aged parents and senior citizens too. I had assumed most of the people attracted to Larry's message were kids in high school and college, but here were people from all age groups settling in for a weekend of music and fun.

People crowded around the entrance gate, but no one seemed impatient or annoyed. Several participants had crossed off the logos on their shirts and jackets, or opted instead for simple handmade T-shirts with "I am not your billboard" stenciled on them. A fifteen-year-old girl asked me if I knew which way to the main stage. Beth had already memorized the map on the drive up and gave her directions.

"This is unbelievable," Beth said for the millionth time. "Larry must be overwhelmed."

I told her that was a pretty safe bet.

Beth's sister and her friends set up camp near the arts and crafts booths. Beth and I carried our tents and sleeping bags down to the body-painting area.

For the first hour, I barely spoke, just stumbled around snapping pictures. My mind reeled from the immensity of the event. Music, colors, food—everything seemed surreal, a Technicolor explosion. Instead of taking credit for Larryfest, patting myself on the back for being the guy who made it all happen, I realized a force much larger than myself at work. The universe was now behind the wheel, and I was all too happy to hand over the driving.

Every few moments, something new caught my eye. Angel wings, tie-dyed togas, horns, fishnets, soccer uniforms, American flags, Dr. Seuss hats, camouflage, Larry tattoos. The food vendors sold the enchiladas, salads, and noodles at cost. Poland Spring gave away thousands of bottles of water. Local bands shared the stage with international stars. The lines at the charity and volunteer-back-home booths rivaled those for the Porta-Johns. People signed petitions, made pledges, sat around campfires, and exchanged ideas. Never in my wildest, most insane dreams could I have come up with something so interesting, so spontaneous, so POSITIVE. Larry had taken on a life of his own.

Beth and I danced for most of the afternoon. When U2 took the stage to close the show Saturday night, the crowd exploded.

Halfway through the set, Bono quieted the masses. "There's been lots of talk about finding out who this Larry really is. Well, I'll tell you, friends—I don't want to know!"

The audience cheered.

"Larry, this one's for you."

The opening chords to what the fans now called "Larry's Theme" filled the night sky.[45] The crowd shouted and sang along. It was, bar none, the greatest moment of my seventeen-year-old life. In the span of an eight-minute song, years of teenage doubts about ever being able to make a difference evaporated. I basked in being a tiny catalyst in the scheme of the universal plan. By the time Beth and I got back to our tents, we collapsed into sleep.

---

[45] To be honest, I would have preferred to hear "Bad," my favorite U2 song, one my mother swore was the greatest rock song ever recorded. But even if Bono had sung "I'm a Little Teapot" I would have screamed just as loudly.

The next day, we sat in on a presentation by the Salt Lake City Larry Organization discussing the way they banned billboards and superstores in their town. The Boulder, Colorado, group coached others on how to fight the gun companies in their state. Billy North had a tent where he discussed his Larry word placement theory.[46] Beth and I joined a group doing yoga in a cathedral of pines. On our way back to camp, we visited several other booths, spending time with two guys from Oakland who were making a video collage about the festival. (I made sure to stay away from the camera.)

Beth wandered ahead for a few minutes, then returned with her hands behind her back. "Ta-da!" She held out a large purple wizard's hat with gold stars and moons. She placed it on my head. "I now pronounce you Josh Swensen, Wizard Extraordinaire."

While part of me figured out which possession I'd have to jettison back home, most of me laughed at the absurdity of her thoughtful gift. Good old Merlin himself couldn't have foreseen a day like this one.

---

[46] I HAD to listen; it was too perfect.

"Do you like it?" Beth asked.

I hugged her close and told her it was fabulous.

We explored the rest of the booths on our way back to the tents.

Wedged in the end of the last row was a cafeteria table with a banner that stopped me in my tracks. SIGN A PETITION FOR LARRY TO FESS UP! I casually approached the table. A clipboard held a large stack of lined paper, most without signatures. A sign on the table explained the petition.

I LIKE WHAT LARRY HAS TO SAY, BUT DOES IT BOTHER ANYONE ELSE THAT HE/SHE IS AFRAID TO SIGN HIS/HER NAME TO HIS/HER SERMONS?

"These people who can't just enjoy things have to find something to bitch about," Beth complained.

SIGN THIS PETITION IF YOU ALSO THINK WE DESERVE TO KNOW WHO THE PERSON IS WHO INVADES OUR HOMES AND MINDS EVERY DAY. SIGN IF YOU BELIEVE THAT THE PHILOSOPHY OF LARRY SHOULDN'T BE ABOUT KEEPING SECRETS.

I didn't need to see who sponsored the petition, but the answer stared back from the page anyway. E-MAIL ME IF YOU WANT TO TALK MORE ABOUT IT. —betagold.

Most of the lines of the petition were filled with things like "Get a life, betagold," or "Who cares? It's working." A few dozen people had signed the petition in support of betagold.

"I wonder if Larry's seen this?" Beth asked. "I wonder what he thinks about it."

"He probably hopes betagold will just go away."

"Well, that makes two of us."

She entwined her hand in mine. I didn't want to put words to it, afraid to break the spell, but in the dreamlike world of Larryfest, Beth and I had suddenly become a couple. Each time my mind turned toward what would happen when we got back home, I pictured a giant red stop sign. I didn't want to ruin the present worrying about the future.

"Let's go back to camp," she said.

My love for Beth hadn't wavered since sixth grade. Now here we were lying in our sleeping bags gazing at the stars, my arm around her in a casual (for her) yet meaningful (for me) way.

The success of the festival had sprung a geyser of giddiness inside me. "So you think Larry's here?" I played with one of her braids while I spoke.

"He's definitely here. And I bet he's *loving* this."

"Oh he is," I said. "Guaranteed."

She propped herself up on her elbow. "What do you think he's like as a person? Some brainwave or just a regular guy?"

"Just another guy in a wizard hat, I'm sure."

She took a long look at me, then punched me in the arm. I pulled her closer to me. To use my Larry-ness as a way of having my way with Beth would be so not-Larry.[47]

If I *were* going to tell Beth about my secret identity, this would be the perfect time. I looked at her cuddled in her sleeping bag and weighed the choices in my mind. YES, NO, YES, NO. YES. NO. YES! Our relationship could reach another level, *I'd* reach another level in the honesty department. And just like that, I decided to tell her.

"Beth?"

"Wait a minute, look." Three girls from Chicago approached us, handing out lyrics to a song they had written for everyone to sing the next morning.

---

[47] Of course that didn't mean a huge part of me didn't want to do just that.

After they left, Beth turned to me. "Yes?"

But the moment had passed. She gave me a squeeze, then lay back to watch the fireworks. She said good night an hour later with a chaste kiss on my cheek. I watched her sleep through the canopy netting.

Did I blow it? Should I have been more assertive, told her how I felt? I was a guy who diagrammed Rubik's Cubes for fun but couldn't dig deep down to that emotional place inside and tell my best friend how I felt about her. I always could do that with Mom, but a person shouldn't be emotionally honest with only one person his whole life, should he? Shouldn't the courtesy extend to everyone? My intentions were good, my feelings were real, but I just couldn't put two and two together. Why don't they make those colorful magnetic numbers for the heart? That's where I *really* needed the help.

Or maybe I was just practicing restraint? Maybe making love to Beth under a sky of fireworks—of all things—would have been gaudy and anticlimactic.[48] Maybe I had done the right thing after all.

---

[48] No pun intended.

I barely slept all night. Some wizard I was—more like Mickey Mouse trying to hold back the flood with buckets. Loser.

I watched the sun rise over the fields of people, then made my way to one of the water stations. A grandmotherly woman dropped her toothbrush in the mud; she seemed ready to cry.

"It's much more crowded than I thought it would be," she said.

I handed her my toothbrush, still in the box. "Here. My friend brought tons of them; she's always overprepared."

The woman grabbed my hand and thanked me profusely. She wore the same hand lotion my mother had always worn. I held my own hand up to my face and inhaled the familiar scent. Mom, I thought, could you ever in a million years have imagined it? The world is shifting, the consciousness is changing, we're evolving in the right direction.

Talk to me, Mom. Tell me what you think. Please.

And then I waited.

The woman in front of me took her place at the makeshift sink. She held up the toothbrush like a flag. "Your mother would be so proud of you."

This woman brushing her teeth would never know how she'd just made my day.

*Critics said it was impossible, but we
    did it!*

*We did it without corporate
    sponsorship.*

We did it without product endorsement.

We did it without burning down tents.

We did it without anger and fights.

We did it without violating women.

We did it without people being afraid.

We did it without cynicism and apathy.

We did it with idealism.

We did it with enthusiasm.

We did it with grassroots efforts.

We did it with hope.

We did it with music.

*We did it even though no one thought
    we could.*

Change the world?

Did.

Are.

Can.

LARRY ITEMS #62 and #67

My feet still hadn't touched the ground when I accessed Larry's messages.

DID YOU HAVE FUN AT LARRYFEST?
DID YOU SEE MY BOOTH?
I ENDED UP GETTING 4,589 SIGNATURES, LARRY. IT'S A REAL MOVEMENT.

I scrolled down; even betagold couldn't scare me today. Or so I thought.

LARRY, IT WOULD BE DIFFICULT, BUT SOMEONE WITH THE RIGHT EQUIPMENT COULD BLOW UP THAT PHOTO, REARRANGE THE PIXELS, AND TRY TO IDENTIFY THE PEOPLE IN IT. I'M NOT GOING TO DO THAT, DON'T NEED TO.
    DID YOU GET A NEW MODEM LINE, LARRY? OR JUST A NEW CELL PHONE WITH A DIFFERENT NUMBER? WHAT'S YOUR PLAN—TO DO THAT

EVERY DAY UNTIL I FIND YOU? NEWS FLASH—
I'M FLYING INTO BOSTON NEXT WEEK TO
TRACK YOU DOWN. YOUR PAL, betagold.

THUD! That would be the sound of my feet
hitting the ground.

On my way to the coffee shop, I wondered who
betagold really was. In my increasing paranoia,
I thought it might be the new waitress. I felt
her eyes on me, but she may have just been
waiting for me to leave so she could wipe down
the table. Betagold had to live in another part
of the country if he or she was flying here,
and whoever it was obviously had enough money
to devote this much time and effort to a game
of cybercat and mouse.

For the next few days at the hardware store,
I did 360-degree spins down the aisles, checking out every angle as I walked. Was it the
man with the flip-up sunglasses buying stakes
for his tomato plants? Was it the girl taking
her time with the plungers? The breeze coming
in the open doors didn't lessen my copious
sweating.

Screw betagold. (Well, not really. I would
still change my modem line even though it was
only three days old.)

No more thinking about quitting.

In hindsight, I should have quit, of course. Closed down the Web site after Larryfest, its greatest success.

But I didn't. I committed myself even further.

I asked myself the eternal question. Fight or flight?

It wasn't a decision.

It was early Saturday afternoon, and I hadn't gotten dressed yet. Beth pointed to my pajama-and-life-jacket ensemble and asked what I was doing.

"I keep having these dreams that I'm drowning," I answered. "Figured I'd go to sleep prepared."

"Dreaming that you're drowning. I wonder what Freud would say."

"Probably some deep-seated emotional problem. And we already know *that's* true." I unbuckled my life vest, slipped it onto Beth's slim frame, and buckled it.

She flipped her long hair back behind her shoulders. "Thanks for saving me," she said.

And right there in my kitchen, I decided to tell her. Tell her I was Larry, that I was trying to save her, save all of us, most of all me. That it would be so much easier to do if she and I were together. I wanted to tell her all about my secret life with the ease of holding open a sleeping bag and letting her climb inside.

But I didn't.

I did something worse.

I kissed her.

"What are you doing?" She jumped away from me so fast I thought she would ricochet out the sliding door.

"I just thought . . . you know . . . after Larryfest . . ."

"That's what I came over to tell you." She moved from the door to the chair to the table. "I'm going out with Todd again."

"What?"

"I was so confused at the festival," she said. "And when I got back, he begged me to come over and talk."

"What about the meat oozing out of his pores?"

"That's what I'm saying. He gave up meat, he's joining the club, we're going to see what happens." Her voice trailed off. "That's why I'm here—to tell you Todd and I are going out." She used her fingers to make quotes around the phrase "going out" to downplay it, make it more ironic. I wanted to reach over and break those piano fingers right off.

She finally stopped babbling and appraised the situation. "I was hoping you'd be happy for me. I mean, just a little."

I could taste the hurt in my mouth—a sweet, metallic taste. But even pain that real didn't translate into honesty. I railed into her instead.

"It's perfect," I continued. "Just what you always wanted. To be dating a big, stupid, meat-eating jock whose chest measurements are almost as large as your IQ."

"You're being ridiculous."

"No, *you're* being ridiculous."

"Look. I thought you could deal with this. I'd crawl into a hole and die if things got weird between us."

"No, we're fine. Just great." *I* was the one who wanted to crawl into a hole and die. Emotionally honest? Guess I still wasn't up to the task.

She unbuckled the life jacket and hung it on the back of the chair. "I know it's a giant cliché and I hate to even say it, but can't . . ."

"If this is about us still being friends, forget it!"

I had never in eight years been truly mad at Beth before. But her insistence on wanting me to be happy that someone else was stealing the girl I'd always loved right out from under me was more than I could bear. I held open the door and told her I had to take a shower.

Could she make this any more torturous?

Of course she could.

She tilted her face to mine and kissed me on the cheek. "Can't we work through this?" she asked. "I'm like your sister, for chrissakes."

Forgive me, I'm an only child, but don't brothers do things like push sisters down flights of stairs? Because that's exactly what I wanted to do—so hard she'd land in the Larsons' yard. I held open the door until she left.

When Peter and Katherine came in from shopping, I barely had the energy to say hello.

"Look what I got!" Katherine's voice was so shrill with excitement it sounded like she'd sucked on a bouquet of helium balloons.

She pulled a Humpty Dumpty candle out of a bag. "Look at the tie he's got on—polka dot to match his little hat! Can you stand it?"

It was extremely difficult to embody Larry's philosophy when what I wanted to do was tell her what a need-a-life psychotic freak she was. I looked over at Peter who smiled as if Katherine had just come up with a cure for cancer while at the local flea market.

"Remember that Larry Web site you and I were talking about?" he asked. "Some guys at the conference are determined to bring this sicko in. These last few ads of his were too much. Talking about workers in Southeast Asia. Those people are lucky they *have* jobs."

"Yeah, we've sold them the idea of the American dream, and now they're going to drop dead working till they get it." I had to get out of here.

Katherine tested various spots around the kitchen, looking for the perfect place for her new candle. "As I told you before, Peter, it's just a matter of time before he gets caught."

Humpty Dumpty's bouncing from shelf to shelf in the kitchen made the whole scene even more surreal. "You can't blame Larry," I said. "There do seem to be a lot of people buying *crap*." My eyes pinned Katherine to the hutch. She hesitated, then moved Humpty to the counter.

I slipped the orange life jacket back on over my pajamas. My dreams were trying to tell me something. I *was* drowning.

Beth and Peter were the two people closest to me in the world, but the feelings of alienation, disgust, and betrayal squeezed me like a vise—so hard that I had to rest on the edge of the living room couch to catch my breath. It doesn't get any worse than this, I thought.

But I was wrong.

When the doorbell rang, I answered it.

A sixtyish woman with gray hair and a floral sundress stood at the door. I smiled at her.

"Can I help you?"

"Are you Josh Swensen?" she asked sweetly.

"Yes."

"You look familiar."

I told her she did too. I tried to register her face. It took several moments, but I did. "I gave you a toothbrush at Larryfest, remember?"

She smiled, taken aback. "You're exactly right. How are you?"

"Fine." What was she doing here?

Beth suddenly appeared from the kitchen. "I came back to see what's going on. There's a camera crew outside."

The older woman answered for me. She turned toward the front lawn. "Let's go, guys!"

Suddenly, the clicking of cameras, the whirring of camcorders filled the room. I noticed the local TV news trucks at the top of the street. The whole scene slowed down as if we were underwater.

"I thought you'd be older," she said. "Thirty, at least." Her grimace indicated my cowlicked morning hair and pajama-lifejacket combo did not meet with her approval.

"Well, Larry, are you going to admit it?"

"I don't know what you're talking about." I tried to shut the front door, but several reporters and cameramen were already inside.

"Josh? What's she talking about?" Beth asked. She glanced at my neck. "When did you get that chain?"

Peter and Katherine entered the room. "What's going on?" Peter asked.

"This boy here, this Josh Swensen is Larry—The Gospel According to Larry."

I swiveled first to Beth, then to Peter. "It's not true. And this chain, I've had it forever. You've seen it a million times."

Peter extended his hand to the woman. "It seems like there's been some kind of misunderstanding. I'm Peter Swensen."

"Josh? What is she talking about?" Beth repeated.

No matter how many times I denied it, if Grandma Nosebag insisted, we could all traipse down to the basement. Nothing incriminating was stored on my hard drive, but the phone with Larry's modem line—that . . . that was sitting right on my desk. I was completely and totally screwed.

The woman shook Peter's hand. "I'm Tracy Hawthorne," she said. "But you can call me . . ."

"Betagold," I answered.

Beth screamed.

What discombobulated me more than anything else was betagold's hand cream. The scent filled the room with memories of my mother. The sound of the cameras clicked like background music as I imagined Mom walking barefoot through the house with her long Indian dress. And this woman, this betagold, had even given me a message from my mother at Larryfest.

Betagold looked me straight in the eye. "I should have recognized you at the festival," she said. "You were the one with the T-shirt and the smile."

PART FOUR

"For what is a man profited, if he shall gain the whole world, and lose his own soul?"

St. Matthew 16:26

GOSPEL ACCORDING TO LARRY—
BOY IN BASEMENT

—San Francisco Examiner

LOCAL TEEN ADMITS HE'S GURU

—Boston Globe

TEEN BASHES AD INDUSTRY

—New York Post

I have a newfound respect for Alice for still being able to function after stepping through the looking glass. When betagold entered our house, it was as if someone reached down to the wall outlet and yanked out the plug connecting my life to anything resembling reality. That afternoon still remains a blur of images: Beth repeatedly shaking betagold's arm, Peter trying to remain diplomatic as his blood pressure soared, Katherine flapping around the room like a dazed chicken.

And the media—poking, prodding, changing my life forever.

Josh Swensen died that day.

I just didn't know it yet.

To be fair, there were a few good points to being outed. Meeting Bono, of course. Lots of other activists from Amnesty International too. A few of us holed up in a hotel room and talked World Bank strategy until the media frenzy got so bad the mayor politely asked me to leave. Also, I didn't have that continual nagging feeling of saying something that would give Larry away. Not having to censor myself for the first time in months was freeing. And I would be lying if I didn't say that at first the attention felt great. I hadn't had that kind of approval since my mother died. Basking in the appreciation of millions of people brought back the feeling I used to get when Mom bestowed one of her roaring laughs as I danced and juggled around the kitchen. Kids from school called and stopped by with hundreds of invitations. This bizarre overfocus soon led to features in the *Boston Globe*, the *New York Post*, even on *Larry King Live*.[49]

As much as I had never wanted the attention, I looked at it this way: Now I could finally spread the word to the millions of people who didn't have access to the Internet. I tried to concentrate on the positive: Larry's anticonsumerism message could reach a whole new audience.

The bad news, however, expanded like a sumo wrestler's waist during training season. Journalists didn't want to know about ending consumerism or being your authentic self. They wanted to know how mad my stepfather was when he found out. They wanted to know if I had a girlfriend and how difficult it was for me after my mother died.

When they asked me to do *20/20*, I naively thought it would be a great way to spread the word.

Unfortunately, Barbara Walters had different ideas. After she grilled me on the boxers/briefs debate, I realized Larry's philosophy had little place in the interview. During a break in the taping, I approached the show's producer.

---

[49] There were way too many "Larry" jokes on that one.

"Why don't you ask me about the Larry clubs across the country, or what people are doing in their towns to slay the corporate giants?"

The producer told me their viewers didn't want to hear about that. "They want to know about you," he said.

"Josh isn't interesting," I responded. "Larry's work—that's the story."

The producer turned to the crew. "Get this—a teenager telling someone with almost fifty years of journalism experience what the story is."

They all laughed, then he turned back to me. "You're the story, just you. People want gossip; people want sizzle."

Barbara smiled for the camera, and we resumed the interview.

All the hours I'd spent honing those sermons and creating those pseudo ads were gone. All anyone cared about now was what kind of breakfast cereal I preferred.[50]

Larry was the new Pokémon, the new Beanie Baby, the new Sony PlayStation.

Larry was now, officially, a product.

And you know what happens to products.

They get consumed.

---

[50] I hate cereal.

I tried to focus on the irony of the situation. For months, my sermons ranted against consuming the lives of celebrities. But after betagold yanked me into the public eye, suddenly every movement of mine made for evening news or tabloid feature.

Flip-Off Phillips called me from her car phone and offered to counsel me and make sure I was okay. I was touched by her concern until she asked me for an autographed photo of the two of us for her wall.

It's not like I was any more welcome at home.

From the second betagold announced my secret identity, Peter went from disbelief to skepticism to outright fury.

"My own stepson—manipulating the minds of millions!"

"Like father, like son."

Thankfully, he let the comment slide. "With information you took from me!"

What could I tell him—that I was curious, that the information looked interesting? That it was the only part of this whole mess I *did* regret?

He suddenly seemed like a balloon deflating before my eyes. "I've lost four of my biggest clients. All because of those ads. People think I'm a traitor!"

"I never wanted to get you in trouble," I said. "I just thought people deserved to see the information."

His usually calm demeanor exploded. "Who are you protecting? Even the Communists are consumers now!"

I might as well have been tied to the back of the chair with the bulb over the kitchen table spotlighting me, interrogation style. Peter's Marine training came back to him, big time. He'd never been captured and sent to a P.O.W. camp, but he was making up for it now. *I* was making up for it.

Each time I tried to explain that I was only voicing my opinion—which I was constitution- ally allowed to do, by the way—he lost it a bit more.

"You're accepting that invitation to *60 Min- utes* and you're telling Mike Wallace you were wrong."

"That buying junk is our moral imperative," I added.

"That's right." He banged his fist on the table so hard, the salt and pepper shakers flew across the room like missiles. He eyed me carefully. "Are you mocking me?"

"No, sir."

"Laugh all you want," he said. "I've been taking care of you for three years; your real father never took care of you for a day." He kept going, on a roll. "He was a real philosopher too. Bumming for quarters on the streets of Cleveland before he drank himself to death."

Never, in all the years I've known him, had Peter been intentionally cruel. But the bent smile on his face gave his perverse pleasure away. When I got up to leave, he pounded the table again. "If you're going to live in this house, you need to retract those sermons and stop all this nonsense."

I took a deep breath. "I can't do that."

"Why? Because you like being famous? Reveling in all this attention?"

I told him I hated the attention, that I had gone to great lengths *not* to be in the spotlight. "I can't help it if we live in a culture that worships people just for being famous."

He shook his head, trying to compose himself. "We might have to move," he said. "Depending on what happens with the rest of my clients."

I couldn't imagine where we could move to and regain our privacy. Fiji? Peru?

"Look," Peter continued. "I appreciate that you're working to make the world a better place. But believe it or not, I am too." He held the edges of the counter for support. "No offense, Josh, but this idealism thing is a phase, like so many others you've been through. Remember the skydiving? The giant Polaroid camera you were obsessed with?"

I told him they were different.

"You say that every time," Peter said. "You don't have enough life experience. You don't know how the real world works yet."

"Adults always say that to keep kids quiet," I said. "You don't have any answers; you're all just muddling through, like the rest of us."

"Unlike you who has all the answers. Right, Mr. Big-Shot Guru?" He grabbed his keys and headed out the door.

I had let myself savor my contributions, but here I was face-to-face with something I had destroyed.

I was suddenly filled with the memory of Peter promising my mother on her deathbed that he would take care of me. And lo and behold, he was living up to his promise. Maybe I should use the *60 Minutes* opportunity to deny Larry's work and bail out Peter.

But I knew I couldn't. Peter's beliefs were an integral part of his life. So were mine. A stalemate—fathers and sons had them all the time. Maybe Peter and I weren't so different from other families after all.[51]

I closed the blinds just as the photographers snapped my picture. I imagined the resulting photographs in tomorrow's newspaper—a seventeen-year-old boy, his body divided by stripes of light, a perpetual prisoner.

---

[51] Except for the photographers hiding out back behind the compost heap—most families didn't have to deal with them. (The temperature had hit 87 degrees; the smell would be horrendous back there. I almost felt bad for them.)

Ahhh, Beth. Beth. Beth.

A few weeks ago at Larryfest, we held hands and chanted about peace and love. Now—post-betagold—she wouldn't even answer the phone. As my best friend, she'd been besieged by the press, with some of the tabloids offering her up to two hundred thousand dollars for an exclusive. She could have paid her entire college tuition with money to spare, but, thankfully, she turned them down.[52]

Needless to say, Beth did not take kindly to finding out my secret identity along with the

---

[52] Her sister Marie unfortunately was not as principled. Always a tattletale, she spilled her guts to whatever newspaper or television show would listen. I heard that one of the tabloids paid her fifty grand for the story of driving Beth and me to Larryfest. I refused to read the article when it hit the stands, but I heard she turned a side-of-the-road whiz into an anecdote involving raccoons, police helicopters, and a startled couple from New Hampshire. Marie always had an active imagination.

rest of the world. The shocked expression on her face as betagold outed me haunts me to this day.

For weeks afterward, my calls and e-mails were not returned. Each time I went to her back door—followed by dozens of paparazzi—her father slammed it closed and told me she wasn't home. I was immediately let go at the hardware store, even though my celebrity had increased sales by over 200 percent.

I waited until a Sunday afternoon when I knew Beth would be doing inventory. As usual, a drum of chlorine propped open the back door to let in the summer air. I stood near the paint-brushes and coughed, so I wouldn't sneak up on her. When she saw me, she smiled.

She tossed me a clipboard and slid a box of washers across the floor. I counted them out as we spoke.

"You could've told me," she said.

I told her I almost did, several times, in fact.

"All this attention would drive the normal person crazy, but you . . ." her voice trailed off. "You must be miserable."

"I never would have done it if I'd known. Never in a million years."

My fingers grew dirtier and more metallic

as I counted; the familiar smell was comforting. Beth wanted to know everything—how I came up with the idea, how I'd kept the site private. "I never once suspected it, even with the Lorax," she said. "But in hindsight, this whole thing is so you." She shook her head. "The Wizard."

She then gave me grief for writing the sermon about phonies. "You posted that one after I bagged you for Todd," she said. "There I was thinking Larry was some kind of genius mind reader, when all along he was the guy next door."

"Hey, Larry had to live next door to *somebody*," I said. "He just lucked out with you."

She smiled, a pre-betagold moment. "It's hard to be friends right now," she said. "I've got to get some perspective on this."

I told her to take whatever time she needed. I had so much more to say, but instead of saying it, I just fidgeted with the new jar openers on the bottom shelf.

"You better go," she said. "My father's coming back in a few minutes. He hasn't been too happy about all of this."

I handed her the washers, all 137 of them.

"So, we'll talk, right?" I asked.

She shrugged. "Soon. Maybe."

I nodded and snuck out the door.

I made sure no one saw me leave, then rode my bike toward the woods. Over the past few weeks, my visits had grown more frequent and extended. If this frenzy didn't die down soon, I'd be setting up camp there permanently.

At this rate, maybe that wasn't such a bad thing.

Believe it or not, it took less than two months for the book deals to kick in. Some enterprising youth downloaded all my sermons and published them in hardcover as *The Larry Bible*. Two unauthorized biographies hit the shelves, one entitled *Josh/Larry—Flip a Coin;* the other, *Messiah in My Homeroom* written by a girl I went to junior high with but never spoke to once. Several acquaintances from my childhood set up their own Web sites. My babysitter from Ohio, where Mom and I lived till I was four, had a popular site called From Pampers to Prophet—Josh Swensen, the Early Years.[53]

One of my biggest disappointments was having to shut down the Web site. Even with the

---

[53] The only thing I remember about this babysitter was that she used to sit on the couch, eat Ho Hos, and do macramé, while I sat on the floor and drew pictures of Gumby and baby Jesus.

latest broadband technology, the site couldn't handle the 255 million hits it now received per day. Worse than that, hardly anyone wanted to discuss issues anymore; the questions posted on the message boards went from "How can we live more meaningful lives?" to "Does anyone know where I can get an XL Larry T-shirt?"

Nike, Tommy Hilfiger, Calvin Klein—all the companies I slammed in my sermons—approached me to endorse their products.

"Does the irony escape you?" I asked the woman who claimed she was from Coca-Cola. "I trash you people for soaking us with advertising and now you want me to represent your product? What kind of philosopher would I be?"

The word *philosopher* almost sent the woman into advertising nirvana. She jumped across the room. "That's it! A heavily rotated commercial—lots of MTV play, lots of fast cuts, girls in short skirts—you're walking down this inner-city street, philosophizing, that's great—hip-hop music blasting in the background—trashing Coke while you're drinking one! It's perfect!"

I pondered the obvious. "Won't people think it's strange that I'm guzzling down a product from a company whose marketing campaign I've detested all along?"

"Is that what you're worried about?" She smiled at me as if I were a two-year-old. "People don't THINK!"

I held open the kitchen door and asked her to leave.

"Ten million dollars." She smiled like the Cheshire cat. "Plus, your stepfather's agency gets the biz."

These advertising people really knew what buttons to push. When Peter found out about her proposal, he played it low key but couldn't help mentioning that the Coca-Cola account was worth more than a billion dollars a year.

I told him I understood, but I still couldn't do it.

I slept under the Larsons' porch so I wouldn't have to deal with Peter again. I felt like a guppy hiding under a piece of coral in an aquarium full of piranhas.

It was only a matter of time before I was swallowed whole.

The next time I saw Beth was out behind the cemetery.[54] She'd e-mailed me to meet her there to avoid the press. I had to leave my house at six in the morning in a long blond wig and fringed jacket not to attract attention.

I thanked the universe for a few moments alone with her.[55]

---

[54] Very fitting considering I wanted to die.

[55] At this point I have to admit that all along I'd day-dreamed about Beth finding out I was Larry. In my reverie, she'd always be shocked at first, then would eventually come around to the idea of the guy next door being her biggest idol. We'd sit in my basement. I'd show her how I'd set up the Web site, read the e-mails only Larry could access, plan the strategy for future sermons. In my dreams, she was my partner, my confidante, my Yoko. Once I imagined a day much like this one, the two of us walking in the woods. In my dream, we sat under a maple and kissed. In one scenario, I uncovered the tarp leading to my subterranean room, and we made love on a bed of leaves until the sun faded below the horizon. Needless to say, this scenario repeated itself in my mind often, most notably during the hours of peeking through the living room curtains waiting for the reporters to leave.

"I just wanted to say goodbye," she said.

When I asked her where she was going, she told me she was spending the rest of the summer at her aunt's.

"Aunt Marge, down the beach?"

"No. Aunt Jo in Seattle."

"What?" Please, don't do this to me. Please.

"This whole year's been crazy. I need to just be alone for a while." She smiled. "I sound like you."

"But then you'll be at Brown. I can see you there, right?"

She pulled some dead ivy off my mother's grave. "Look, friendship is based on honesty. And let's face it, you were living a giant lie."

I cajoled, I begged, I offered a thousand excuses. She stood firm.[56]

"You know me. Hypocrites drive me insane. And the world's gone completely nuts over this. Betagold sells you out, and what does she get? A million-dollar book deal and a prime-time special. To say nothing of that stupid tooth-

---

[56] Which unfortunately for me had always been her finest quality.

brush she's charging people to see.[57] You'd think it was the Ark of the freaking Covenant."

"No one wants to talk about Larry's message anymore," I complained. "About how we're wasting natural resources, exploiting workers ..."

"You don't have to summarize Larry's philosophy for me," Beth snapped. "I know it as well as anyone."

"Of course you do."

"Let's face it, Josh. Half of those rants were mine. The World Bank screwing Third World countries? I wrote a paper on that for Mr. Bartlett's class. I'm glad you got the word out to others, but let's not pretend you're some kind of expert here."

She did that quotation-mark thing around the word *expert*. I felt my face redden and looked down, only to get fixated on her tattoo peeking out from the hem of her jeans. Our relationship had deteriorated so much in the past month, I would never dare to reach over and touch it anymore. Instead I asked her what happened with Todd.

She sighed. "It was stupid to think we could

---

[57] A shocked pilgrim had e-mailed me betagold's brochure—$100 to see the toothbrush, $500 to hold it, and $3,000 to actually use it. Scary.

be a couple," she said. "We had nothing in common at all."

"*We* had something in common," I said. "*We* should've been the couple."

"Yeah, well too late now, isn't it?"

I looked into her eyes, confused.

"You're not saying you thought about it too, are you?"

Her lack of response sent me to my feet.

"Don't do this to me! After all I've been through, don't pull this on me now!" I shouted. "Are you saying you *wanted* us to be together? All this time?"

She concentrated on a patch of moss near the tombstone. "Just since ninth grade."

I stomped through the graveyard repeating the word *NO* over and over. "This is not happening, this can't possibly be happening . . ."

My feelings ricocheted between fury and hope, if that's possible. Maybe we could still salvage something from all this wasted time.

But my dream scenario barely kicked into first gear before Beth interrupted it.

"We should just end it," she said. "Besides, I need to get out of here. I was turning into too much of a conformist, following Larry's every word. I'll be better off on my own program, contributing on a more personal level."

She ran her hand along the top of the tombstone. "Bye, Mrs. Swensen." She turned to me. "Bye, Josh."

And, just like that, the girl I had loved forever walked out of my life.

"You can't go!" I shouted. "We never even tried!"

"Goodbye, Larry."

"I'm not Larry; I'm Josh. It's me! Goddamn it, stop!"

But she didn't.

Could I possibly be a bigger wimp? Not able to cough up enough of my real feelings until it was too late. Betagold was right. I was the worst kind of philosopher—a coward, a man (hardly) of ideas not rooted in anything real, anything from the heart. A voice inside me screamed not to let her go. But I did.

I slumped against my mother's tombstone, my future residence for all eternity. "Mom?"

She didn't answer. The only noise I heard was the distant roar of a small plane overhead. It towed a colorful banner that read LARRY DRINKS MOUNTAIN DEW.[58]

---

[58] It appeared that companies didn't even NEED my endorsements anymore; they just did what they wanted anyway.

I rolled over into the dirt, covered my eyes and ears like a baby. I'd lost Beth and destroyed Peter, my privacy, and my vocation, all in one fell swoop. Not much going on for Josh in the plus column these days.

I stared at the brown earth until I felt human again.

Which took me until the next morning.

I sat on the couch and munched on my third bag of potato chips. Beth's absence in my life left a void wide enough to drive an eighteen-wheeler through. I knew the emptiness would be with me for a very long time.

Meanwhile, Peter had begged me to make a statement that I had come up with the pseudo ads on my own, that he knew nothing about them. I did, but that didn't stop the backlash. He lost several more clients but refused to fold the company. One thing about Peter—he was a pro. Make it work, or die trying.

I documented the media circus as much as I could, taking photos of the reporters taking photos of me. Even that got old after a while. Between no job and no Beth, I had nothing to do but sit around in clothes I'd worn for days and channel surf. My brain simmered in my head like overcooked squash.

One "expert" on the *Today* show—a Swiss psychiatrist—interpreted the drawing of a preschooler. The picture didn't look familiar at all, yet the gentleman explained that Josh/Larry had painted it in 1987 at the Little Red Wagon Preschool. (Some enterprising teacher had scoured the preschool archives hoping for a quick buck, I guess.)

The psychiatrist explained that the birds and sun in the painting led him to believe that Josh/Larry had been a happy child, but the crooked window on the left side of the house pointed to an ominous future.

I threw down my chips, dialed New York City information, and got the studio's number. They didn't even bother to verify if I was the "real" Larry—ratings, ratings—they just put me through. My voice bounced from the phone to the TV. "I never made those birds that look like *V*s," I told the psychiatrist. "That's the lazy way to draw a bird."

Inside the television, on the other side of the room, the doctor shook his head. "Denial," he said. "I should have known denial would be an issue, from the missing bricks in the chimney."

I slammed down the phone, disgusted.

Trapped.

Bored.

Misunderstood.

Overanalyzed.

Hated.

Worshipped.

Friendless.

And worst of all—noncontributing.

I had to get out of here.

When Gus, the mailman, dropped off the five bags of that day's mail, I pulled him inside. I tore off my T-shirt, wrote my name on a piece of paper, and handed it to him.

"You can get three hundred dollars for this on e-Bay," I said. "Just let me borrow your uniform for an hour."

No moral dilemma for Gus; he yanked off his jacket quicker than you could say "Parcel Post."

With Gus's hat pulled down over my face, I strode out of the house and past the media stationed at the bottom of the street.[59] I pretended to deliver mail to the Larsons, then walked quickly to the main road.

---

[59] Peter's attorneys had fortunately gotten restraining orders to keep them away from the property.

At the 7-Eleven, I jumped on the bus to Chestnut Hill.

Twenty minutes later, I collapsed on the stool at the Bloomingdale's makeup counter. I had to hurry; even in the postal uniform, I'd be recognized soon.

"Mom, it's all screwed up," I sobbed. "Nothing's changed at all. I thought I was *contributing*." The new Chanel woman seemed afraid enough of my ranting to stay behind the counter.

"Mom, tell me what to do."

And I did what I always did. I waited.

Two women, each weighed down with armloads of upscale shopping bags, walked toward me.

"Talk to me, Mom."

And my mother answered me loud and clear through one of these meticulously made-up women.

"Sometimes I could just kill myself," the woman told her friend.

I looked up toward the ceiling. "Mom?"

The shopaholic stood next to me and sprayed her wrist with perfume. "I'm completely serious. Sometimes it's the only way."

Even my connection with Mom was gone.

I miss you, Mom, but not enough to join you. Sorry.

The universe, however, sent me several hints to let me know the option should at least be considered.

First off, I went through an old book Beth had lent me—back in ancient times months ago when we were still friends. Inside, marking a page, was the tarot card of the skeleton in the boat.

Secondly, the photographs I'd taken at the cemetery kept turning up. In my desk drawer, under my bed. I ran my finger over the prints, touching the glossy granite as if I were back at the gravesite itself. Was my name on the stone some kind of premonition? I gathered the photos together and shoved them in the bottom of my closet.

I waited till most of the press had left for lunch, then jumped on my bike. Destination unknown, just pedaling furiously out of town in the rain.

I'm not supposed to kill myself! Things had gotten so out of hand that even my regular communication with Mom was off. The signals crossed—she would never have given me that kind of advice.

I pedaled for several hours, toward the ocean, toward anywhere. To prove how insane the suicide idea actually was, I headed toward the Sagamore Bridge. Several people had jumped from its heights; I'd just look and see how impossible the whole idea really was.

Even with the rain and howling wind, I felt content for the first time in weeks. Alone at last, leaving everyone behind. For someone who coveted his privacy as much as I did, the whole Larry feeding frenzy was worse than a nightmare. The part of my life that grounded and nurtured me—my solitude—had been stolen away, leaving me with no other options to access that safe, quiet place inside. Would the brouhaha ever die down? Would I ever get my life back? As each day went by, that option seemed less and less likely.

I'd crossed the Sagamore before but never on my bike. The wind ripped through the cables on the narrow pedestrian path. Rush hour had already begun.[60] If I were going to kill myself—which I wasn't—I'd have to pick a better time than this.

I walked my bike toward the center of the bridge, leaned it against a piling, then looked down.

It was a cold and scary trajectory.

And there was NO way in the world, EVER in a million years, that I could jump off a bridge like this one.

Part of me was happy, of course. I mean, who wants to die? But the part of me that had furiously pedaled here in the rain, that part of me felt vaguely disappointed that another option had been crossed off the list. Now that suicide was out, how was I going to get out of this mess? As dusk took over the sky, I realized the rain had stopped long ago. What I kept wiping from my eyes were tears.

---

[60] Why do they call it rush hour when the cars are not rushing and it lasts much longer than an hour?

The clincher came the very next day while I sat on my bed working with Greek and Latin roots.[61] *Ped* for "foot," *homo* for "man," to "nym" just a few. I sat with the dictionary in front of me, coming up with as many words as I could to pass the time.

Pedestrian, homicide, pseudonym . . . I had more than seventy-two of them. Then, by accident — so I thought — I connected two halves that didn't seem like a word until I looked it up online.

Pseudo-, "false," and *-cide*, "killing." *Pseudocide*. To pretend to kill yourself.

I stared at the word for a good long time. *Homicide, suicide, genocide:* these were words you could find in the newspaper every day. But *pseudocide* . . . I'd been through these roots a

---

[61] School was over, I was starting Princeton in a month, and I was doing Advanced English for fun. What a nerd.

thousand times and never made this particular combination until now. (My pseudo ads were part of what had gotten me into this whole mess to begin with.)

My mind wandered back to yesterday's excursion to the Sagamore Bridge. Suppose I didn't kill myself but *pretended* to? Would the media onslaught finally die down? Would I be able to emerge six months later when the planet had moved on to the next flavor of the month? It was something to think about, a spin on Mom's idea that just might work. There was a world of difference between killing yourself and pretending to kill yourself, and the difference would be my life. Getting my life back by giving it up—it made about as much sense as anything else had lately.

Pseudocide. A way to start again as someone else, to burn the old self and try on a new one. It's not like I was doing the world any good being Josh OR Larry these days.

I erased the word from my notebook; it was a word I wanted to savor, to keep to myself for a while.

When I was little, I adored *Tom Sawyer*. I read and reread the part about Tom and Huck attending their own funeral—listening in while everyone sang their praises, the looks of surprise on Becky's and Aunt Polly's faces when the minister spotted Tom and Huck upstairs.

Dying yet not dying.

It was something to think about.

The plan would have to be multilayered, of course; I mean, if someone were *really* going to pretend to kill himself, he'd need a new identity and city to live in, money, of course . . . I pulled out my laptop and began to make notes. Purely hypothetical.

By two-thirty the next morning, I had eleven pages of ideas and three pages of research that needed to be done. I called it Project Tom Sawyer just for laughs.

As I got ready for bed, I wondered if this was just another Josh Swensen can-this-plan-possibly-be-implemented exercise or if I was actually thinking about doing it. I didn't need to look too far for an answer. Just like finding *pseudocide* in the online dictionary, the sign I was searching for came from the words themselves.

The first pages of ideas began with *he* and *someone.*

The last few pages all began with *I.*

PART FIVE

"For as yet they knew not the scripture,
that he must rise again from the dead."

St. John 20:9

The next day I jumped out of bed with my old energy—finally a new project to throw myself into. I probably wouldn't go through with it, but I had to admit, having such a huge list of obstacles to overcome was a giant turn-on.

I thought about the list of past lives Beth and I had made in homeroom. Forget a past life; I was ready to create a future one.

What would be the best way to die—hypothetically, of course? Drug overdose? Street fight? No, it couldn't be anything where a body was needed; then I wouldn't be able to return after the whole ordeal blew over. Lost or missing wouldn't work; the media would never give up looking for me. Everyone would need to think I was really dead. My mind continually returned to drowning. Maybe the ocean, not some lake or pond they could easily dredge.[62] My recurring dream, the life jacket, the skeleton in the boat all pointed to drowning. I looked at it as a baptism of sorts.

In the end I decided to go with my instincts. Why complicate things? And as scary as the Sagamore had been, it met all the necessary requirements. With the strong currents and winds of the Cape Cod Canal, a body would soon disappear into the arms of the Atlantic. I grinned like a newborn, and in a way I was.

I spent days on the Internet. I looked through phone books and travel magazines. I searched newspaper archives.[63] It was nice to keep busy for a change.

I made another to-do list: register my bicycle with the police department; begin taking early-morning marathon bike rides to establish the habit; get a new post office box; purchase hair dye, scissors, and glasses; send away for vacation brochures from the towns on my list; contact several town halls for birth certificates; quietly sell a few stocks in my portfolio. All these steps had to be accom-

---

[62] This whole plan would be impossible if Mom were still here; she'd empty the ocean with coffee cups if she had to, to make sure I wasn't still alive.

[63] Do you know they're called "morgues"?

plished without alerting the press, a tall order indeed.

The way my blood surged through me reminded me of the buzz I got when I first began the Larry site—the anticipation, the enthusiasm. I would need the skill of a high-wire acrobat to pull the whole thing off, but that was part of the appeal.

My death became the act I'd been rehearsing for my whole life.

There'd be lots of news coverage—and I use the word *news* lightly—then eventually the story would die down. My plan would decimate Peter, of course, but I was almost beginning to think he'd be better off without me. Maybe in his grief, his clients would finally forgive him, and he could build his business back up. The other night he sat me down at the kitchen table with a stack of eight-by-ten glossies and a felt-tip pen. He'd been drinking. He said the guys at the latest conference had been bugging him for autographs. Not for them, of course; Larry was the enemy, but what about their kids? The photos were reprints of me mowing the lawn last summer. He shoved the pen into my hand. "At least I'll be able to pay the mortgage this month," he said. "A for-profit prophet." He laughed at his own joke, spilling his Scotch.

I signed the photos.

Although Beth had made a full-time job out of ignoring me lately, she'd probably take my "death" hard too.[64] But my good thoughts outweighed the bad. I'd get to spend several months either hiding out in the woods or traveling cross-country. With glasses, different color hair, and a low profile, I should be able to move around the nation undisturbed, my precious solitude returned. Being able to be just Josh again would be worth it. Technically, I couldn't be Josh, of course, but being anyone these days was better than being Josh OR Larry.

I still wasn't going to go through with it. It was a task to focus on, to keep me busy during the empty, lonely summer. Just for fun, I chose a day Peter would be out of town. I marked D day on my mental calendar.

D for Destiny.

D for Death.

---

[64] I had mixed feelings about this: I didn't want her to be hurt, yet on the other hand I hoped she would be. Not because I wanted revenge, but because I harbored the hope she still cared.

I worked around the clock, taking only short breaks to unwind by whiting-out comic strips and making up my own dialogue. I went back and forth on the suicide note decision: If I left a note, how would I explain it when I returned? That I survived the 135-foot fall and swam to shore? Unlikely. Besides, couldn't most people figure out why I'd want to kill myself WITHOUT a note? If I didn't leave one, more options opened up. I could return in a few months and say I never *did* jump off the bridge, that someone knocked me from my bike and I wandered around with no recollection of who I was.[65] Peter didn't have an insurance policy on me, so there could be no accusation of fraud. As the weeks went by, I sold off a few of the stocks

---

[65] By then I would have grown my hair out back to brown and no one would be the wiser.

Mom had left me; the profit was enough for me to live frugally for several months.

I received copies of three birth certificates at my new post office box. They were from guys about my age who had died from various causes in cities across the country.[66] With the birth certificates, I got copies of their Social Security numbers, and with both forms of ID, I obtained three different driver licenses from nearby states. I'd be able to go from one identity to the other whenever necessary.

The actual "suicide" played like a movie in my mind. I'd need every bit of drama I could muster to pull it off. (If I were going to do it, which I wasn't.) I chanted Larry's words in my head like a mantra—BE THE HERO OF YOUR OWN LIFE, BE THE HERO OF YOUR OWN LIFE.

It was nice to have advice from somebody you trusted.

---

[66] I got all the relevant information from the newspapers—names of both parents, date of birth. The mother's maiden name was key.

I'd spent more than six weeks assembling all the various information someone who was dropping out would need, but was I being honest with myself? As D day approached, I had to face the fact that a tiny part of me was actually thinking about going through with this crazy plan. Sure, I loved intricate plots as much as the next person, but this one was more serious than any of my other hoaxes. There was only one thing to do—a vision quest.

I had used my pit in the earth for a vision quest once before. After my mom died, I told Peter I was camping but came out to the woods for several days of fasting, prayer, and thought. The Native Americans were big on spiritual transformation through solitude; I was hoping if it worked for them, it would work for me. By the time I came out three days later, I could actually live alongside my grief.

So now I sat in my sacred place once again, trying to come to terms with my pain. The first day, my mind was consumed with the mundane—how long had it been since I'd eaten? How much time had passed? Had it rained? By the second day, the chatter subsided, leaving me to deal with the bigger questions.

Who was Josh Swensen anyway? And why did he need to create Larry to spout his opinions? Didn't he trust his own voice? I realized I was thinking of myself in the third person again—why? Why did I have such a hard time embracing "I," just being Josh? Did everyone else my age have this problem too?

I stared at the almost-full moon overhead. I chanted. I prayed. I huddled in my blanket. I waited.

In my altered state, I recalled a biblical coloring book someone had given to me when I was a kid. The image in my mind was captioned "The Agony in the Garden"—Jesus in Gethsemane, his expression lonely, full of suffering and doubt. Contrary to popular opinion, I'd never considered myself a god, not even with a small g. But lonely, suffering, and full of doubt? That hit the proverbial nail on the head—or cross, as the case may be.

Other pictures in the coloring book flashed before me—the Crucifixion, the Resurrection. How had I gone from being a kid lying on the kitchen floor with a box of crayons to a boy sitting in a hole in the woods contemplating his own death? Did I miss something? Anything?

As the second night turned to day, then night again, I remembered what I'd read about Native Americans on vision quests. They either died, came back crazy, returned home, or disappeared without a trace. Those were the only options.

On the afternoon of the fourth day, I emerged from my pit, squinted up at the sun, and knew which option was mine.

On the appointed day, I jumped out of bed from a fitful sleep, not refreshed but full of an anxious excitement. I showered and dressed quickly, took a look around my room to see if I'd forgotten anything. I said goodbye to my sixty-three possessions. (The other twelve were coming with me.) I walked around the house, past the paisley chair my mom used to read in, past the Humpty Dumpty candle Katherine had insinuated onto the counter, past Peter's stack of *Fortune* and *Business Weeks*. I guess I was a lot like him after all—make it work, or die trying.

I wouldn't be honest if I said I didn't think about calling the whole thing off, but that thought came and went like any other. I tightened the hood of my sweatshirt to cover my newly shorn and dyed locks, grabbed my pack, and left.

No one from the neighborhood saw me; it was two-thirty, and Mr. Munroe—the earliest guy to tool off to the rat race—didn't usually leave till six. My pace was relaxed, almost slow motion.

When my mother pulled me in the wagon back in Ohio, we used to wander around the neighborhood and sing, "Hello, stop sign. Hello, German shepherd." She used to stop the wagon sometimes and turn to me with her hands on her hips, laughing. "Hello, my Joshie." Today, I played the game in a strange nighttime reverse. "Goodbye, mailbox. Goodbye, fence. Goodbye, Josh Swensen."

On the long ride to the bridge, I didn't pass many cars. The Samaritan sign at the base of the bridge implored the desperate to call for help. There was still time to change my mind. I didn't.

I lifted my bike every few feet on the grating, peering down to choppy water below. If I were really going to kill myself, this would be one ballsy way to do it.

I pulled my bike against one of the gray girders near the middle of the bridge. I looked long and hard to make sure no one was driving or jogging, then I kicked off my sneakers and sweatshirt and tossed them into the water. Fast as lightning, I tore off my jeans—Josh's jeans, Larry's jeans—and stuffed them into my pack. In my running shorts, I put on the new glasses and running shoes, then waited for the next car. I felt like I was going to throw up. The sweat I had going was a bonus; it made my running disguise all the better.

After a few minutes, a Volvo headed toward me with a station wagon close behind. Half crazy with fear, I flagged them both over.

"Some guy just jumped! I ran across the bridge and tried to stop him, but he didn't listen!"

The man in the Volvo got out and looked at the bike propped against the side of the bridge. "Was it a kid?"

"Maybe eighteen or so. By the time I got close, he jumped."

The man reached inside the car for his cell phone and dialed 911. The couple in the station wagon approached. "Is everything okay?" the woman asked.

"Some kid, some stupid kid jumped!" I paced back and forth between the three of them, my nervousness real. "I can't deal with this. I've got to get out of here."

"You should at least tell the police what

you saw," the Volvo guy said. He moved closer to the bike, not touching anything. One good thing about all those cop shows; anybody who watches TV knows how to deal with a crime scene. "Looks like this bike is registered; maybe the police can track it down."

More and more cars pulled over; a wave of panic rushed over me that even in my disguise someone would recognize me. One guy in a pickup punctuated the darkness with his horn. The station wagon woman looked at me. "How traumatic—out for a run and someone kills himself right in front of you."

I knew I would feel a lot of pressure during this part of the plan; I hadn't realized how physical the nervousness would be. I ran to the edge of the bridge and threw up, last night's dinner following the path of my sneakers and sweatshirt.

The woman handed me a wad of tissues from her purse. "You should go," she said. "You're just a youngster yourself."

I picked up my pack just in time to see two police cars weave their way across the bridge. The guy in the Volvo approached the cop driving the first car. He pointed straight at me.

"This kid was out for a run and saw a guy get off this bike and jump."

The officer looked at me as if to verify the statement. I pushed my glasses up my nose and nodded. "I ran as fast as I could, but I couldn't get to him in time."

The Volvo guy led the two cops to the bike. "Looks like the jumper's registered his bike."

The cop turned to me. "Can you describe him?"

"Gray sweatshirt, hood pulled tight around his face, jeans, sneakers. About the same height as you are." I wanted to avoid all comparisons to myself.

"And your name is?"

"Gil Jackson. I've been camping here this week." Don't be too eager, I thought. He'll ask you again if he needs anything.

He moved on to the Volvo guy and the people in the station wagon. I caught a small corner of Josh's jeans peeking out of my pack. I nonchalantly zipped it as I waited for the police to finish.

Suddenly, a truck from a local TV station made its way down the bridge. People started getting out of their cars; more people beeped their horns. I asked the cop if I could go.

"I need a number where I can get in touch with you if I have to."

"I'm leaving for L.A. tonight. If you give me your card I'll call you when I settle in."

The detective gave me a long look, then handed over his card. He took the number of the Volvo guy.

A woman followed by a cameraman ran toward us. Any reporter might recognize me, disguised or not.

"I feel like I'm going to be sick again." I headed to the edge of the bridge, listening to the cops talk with the reporters. By now there were twenty or so people peering down into the water, as if the body—my body—would suddenly pop up and appear. I excused myself through the crowd, moving farther away from the scene.

"Hey, what's going on up there?" a guy asked from his Beetle.

"Someone jumped."

"No kidding!" He turned to the woman next to him. "Annie, check this out!"

The woman bolted out of the car with her videocamera, ready to join in the circus.

I eyed the crowd, the police, my bike. It came down, as it always did, to a visceral decision.

I never looked back.

PART SIX

"And when they found not his body, they came, saying, that they had also seen a vision of angels, which said that he was alive. . . . And their eyes were opened, and they knew him; and he vanished out of their sight."

St. Luke 24:23, 31

One of the benefits of living near a large city
is that you can hide out, still be close to
things, and stay incognito. I checked into the
Shady Time Motel in a suburb north of Boston
for one reason: to watch the hullabaloo of
Josh/Larry's suicide. The bike registration
and Gil's eyewitness account would be the pri-
mary means of identification. The bike would
also save a few days of tracking—for Peter's
benefit, as well as my own. By the middle of
the morning, the police had tracked Peter down
in Chicago; he grabbed the next flight and was
back in Boston by six.

Even the all-invasive television coverage
couldn't document Peter's most private moments
(not that they didn't try). I imagined the
scene as if in a movie: Peter, head in hands,
sitting on my bed, berating himself, the word
why? echoing off the walls of the room like a
bullet. Katherine would gently blot her eyes

so her mascara didn't run and tell him there's no way he could have known. The melodrama of the scene almost sent me reaching for the phone several times. But I told myself the situation was temporary, that I just needed to hold on.

They interrupted the local shows to cover the gruesome details of my death. One reporter stood outside the empty high school droning on about my life.[67] He had rounded up several students and teachers to come out for their fifteen minutes of fame. Ms. Phillips spoke about my early admission to Princeton, and Mr. Gibbons, about my talent in physics and photography. Debbie Holden, who never did anything but ignore me, cried so hard into the camera they had to cut to the parking lot for the reporter to finish talking. CNN ran live coverage of the canal search—the Coast Guard trawlers, the crowds on the bridge. They'd turned up one sneaker, which Peter ID'd as mine.[68] The whole thing gave me the creeps. I jumped a foot off the bed when I caught a

---

[67] He actually had the nerve to quote Larry: "Such a shame. Such a waste. He was such a lovely boy."

[68] The photograph of the lone shoe eventually made its way across the Internet and onto 16 million T-shirts. The shoe itself ended up in a glass case at the Ripley's Believe It or Not Museum.

glimpse of myself in the motel mirror; the short blond hair made it seem like someone else had entered the room. Maybe someone had.

I tried not to hate betagold, tried to listen to the Larry part of me and understand her point of view. She held a press conference saying my suicide was not her fault, that Larry belonged to the people in life and in death. She felt sorry for Josh's family and Larry's fans, but it was her "duty and destiny" to bring Larry to the public.[69]

Over the next few days, I ate take-out salads and ice-cream sandwiches and watched CNN nonstop. It wasn't just the what-will-they-say-about-me-when-I'm-gone curiosity, although that was partly it. Mostly I wanted to make sure there were no doubts about the suicide. If the detectives thought anything was suspicious, if Peter refused to believe the evidence, if they kept the case open, my plan would be a resounding failure.[70]

BUT if they all believed Josh/Larry was

---

[69] She actually said, "Outing him was my gift to the cosmos." Get a grip.

[70] My worst fear: The detectives rule out suicide and the world goes on a crazed Larry hunt. Like poor Elvis, the public would feast on me even in death. It was a recurring nightmare that woke me in a full sweat on many occasions.

dead, if they held the memorial service, if no one suspected anything, I could reappear with my alibi six months later and go back to being Josh again. I practiced my story repeatedly to make sure it sounded authentic: A guy jumped me, tossed me from my bike, and rode off. I wandered around the Cape until a man finally gave me a lift. I passed out in his car, then woke up at his house in Connecticut and couldn't remember my name. I left after a few days and wandered around till my memory slowly returned. That's when I'd quietly appear at Peter's—or maybe somewhere else. I still wasn't sure.

The detectives checked every airline and train to L.A. to question Gil Jackson again. As part of the plan, I'd purchased a ticket as Gil on an unreserved train so no one could tell if he'd used it or not. They sent out several requests on L.A. radio stations for Gil to come forward for further questioning. Given Peter's testimony about my bike rides to the Cape and how miserable I'd been, the detectives finally gave up trying to find Gil. The last person to see Josh alive was as fictitious a character as Larry himself.

I'd purposely left my laptop and camera at home for one reason. If the police did think this whole "suicide" was a ploy, Peter would testify that there was no way I would have left either of them behind. I watched a clip of Peter on the six o'clock news telling reporters I wouldn't go out to breakfast without my camera or laptop, never mind running away. One eager-beaver detective noticed I'd sold a few of my stocks over the past few months. That led to a flurry of speculation that I had disappeared with the money. Thinking this might happen, I had also left several letters from the Red Cross, the American Cancer Society, and other charities thanking me for my recent donations. (I'd written most of the letters myself. Some of the contributions were real, of course, but I'd also done some hacking into their fundraising databases and made myself look more philanthropic than I was.) So Josh was finally left alone and given the official stamp of suicide. Peter scheduled the memorial service for the next day.

I sat on the orange motel bedspread and turned on the TV. When I saw the crowds lined up for miles, I thought someone had just assassinated the Pope. To my horror, the crowd was assembled outside my mother's cemetery. After several teachers and "friends" eulogized me, I was shocked to see Beth take the podium. She had seamlessly moved from Seattle to Providence to start her freshman year at Brown. I felt bad throwing this at her so soon after school started. But she spoke confidently into the microphone, her face filling the several jumbo monitors behind my empty coffin.

"Josh Swensen became Larry for one reason—to contribute to the world. He believed we as humans were an endangered species, that the predators who would lead to our demise were ourselves. He had a laser-like mind that focused on one thing—looking inside instead of outside ourselves for answers. He was right about a lot of things. I wish he hadn't been right about our insatiable hunger for the new and exciting. I wish he hadn't been right about how far we'd go to keep ourselves entertained. He would have hated this circus today. He was a boy who swung on swings, who could do the Python's Silly Walk routine verbatim, who wanted nothing less of himself than to change the world. We lost someone amazing today, but we're all too amused by the spectacle to know it."

She left the stage and disappeared into the crowd.

I paced around the room in a panic—Beth! So eloquent, so powerful! I wanted to race to the cemetery and jump on her like the old days. The only thing making this forced exile bearable at all was the thought of seeing her again in a few months. If I could hold it together until then, surely she'd be open to being friends again. At this point I would have settled for sitting on her front steps one more time watching the Petersons' Christmas lights flicker on and off.

But my elation at the idea of a renewed life with Beth quickly dissipated when I saw the JumboTron images of Peter. He pushed the grave diggers away and threw shovelful after shovelful of dirt himself. I burst into tears, deeply sorry for his pain and suffering. His movements reminded me of all the hours I'd spent digging my hole in the woods, and suddenly we didn't seem like we were on opposite sides at all. Remorse filled the room like a musty bedspread.

I wasn't happy with the situation, but I couldn't turn back now. The next day I would check out, head west for a while, and do what all pilgrims do.

Wait for a sign.

Most people don't get the chance to visit their own grave site, so it seemed like a waste not to take advantage of these unusual events and grieve for myself at the cemetery. The dyed hair, hat, and glasses were a must since hundreds of people still milled around the gates and tombstone. When I finally had a chance to get close enough, the picture I'd had in my mind for months became a reality: JOSHUA SWENSEN 1983-2001. The letters and numbers were etched deep into the granite, matching my mom's perfectly. All these people who had brought flowers and cards, who sat on the grass singing and praying, none of them knew my mother, none of them knew *me*. Didn't they have people in their own lives to love? If Larry was here, he surely would have written a sermon about it.

I wondered if Mom was watching; I listened

for her energy but heard nothing. I sat against a large maple with several of its leaves already on the ground. One thing about pretending to die—you missed out on the whole life-flashing-before-your-eyes thing. The images floated by now—Mom pushing me on a swing at the old neighborhood playground, selling lemonade and fortune cookies in front of our house during the summer, Mom bringing Peter to my fencing lesson to meet me for the first time, Beth getting yelled at for passing me *Mad* magazine during Social Studies, Mom and Peter exchanging vows on the beach in Jamaica, Beth grabbing my hand during the rerelease of *The Exorcist* and not letting go till the parking lot, Mom not having the strength to open the car door after her chemo treatments. Images, memories, thoughts—they were the only real possessions any of us had anyway.

The last thing I had to do before leaving town was risky, but inevitable. I walked for miles on back roads till I got to the street behind Beth's. Under cover of twilight, I snuck into the Hamlins' yard and hid behind their overgrown rhododendron and waited. After a few hours, Beth came out as she often did, to sit on her front steps. She wore shorts and her shirt from the hardware store with *Beth* embroidered on the left breast pocket.[71] Did she miss me? Or had she banished me from her heart months ago? From the opposite side of the street, we watched the arc of the Petersons' sprinkler in silence. Everything she'd been through showed on her face—she seemed more mature and determined. I loved her more than I ever had in my life.

Eventually she went inside. I came out from my hiding place[72] and headed back to the motel. Tomorrow I would buy a ticket to Santa Fe as Thomas Patton, yet another of Josh's alter egos.

Was it worth it? If I had Larry to do all over again, would I? These were questions I asked myself often and still wasn't sure about the answers. But was the whole thing worth losing myself over, even temporarily? I think it was. I'd made mistakes, of course: caring more about my message than about the people in my life. Next time out I'd try to find a better balance.

---

[71] I had wanted to take mine with me, but it's hard to travel incognito wearing a shirt that says *Josh*.

[72] Ollie, Ollie, oxen free. Right, betagold?

There were other lessons too; I just hadn't learned them yet.

I got some Chinese takeout and sat in the park down the street from the motel.

Goodbye, Massachusetts.

Tom is hitting the road.

On my way out of town the next day, I stopped at a small Kinko's on the outskirts of the city to check out the Internet.[73]

It was a mistake.

A GIANT mistake.

I checked the *Boston Globe* Web site for any major news. The headline grabbed me by the shirt and threw me across the room.

PATERNITY SUIT FILED AGAINST DEAD PHIL-OSOPHER.

I clicked on the article; maybe they were talking about Kierkegaard.

But sure enough, Josh Swensen, blah, blah, blah.

Some girl from Idaho (where I've never been) . . .

Claiming sex (WHICH I'VE NEVER HAD!) . . .

---

[73] It had been almost a week, after all. I was entitled.

In the back of a Toyota pickup (which I've never driven).

Can you slander a dead man?

Can you slander a man PRETENDING to be dead?

Every fiber of my being hoped this was an isolated incident.

It wasn't.

I slept in my hole in the woods most nights and ventured out to the newsstands in the early mornings.

If I weren't already dead, I'd want to be now, believe me.

I thought it couldn't get any worse.

I was wrong.

Sixteen different men came forward saying they were my real father. I read all their profiles with interest, but none of the statistics matched my poor old dead alcoholic dad.

Then the conspiracy theories started coming out of the woodwork. Larry was one of the masterminds behind the 1995 Oklahoma bombing.[74] Larry stalked child stars in Hollywood. I laughed—hysterically—at the first several

---

[74] Apparently no one seemed to mind that I was eleven at the time.

theories, but soon the weight of the lies buried what was left of my spirit. I had started out writing sermons about the toxic effects of celebrity worship and accumulation; never in my wildest dreams could I have envisioned that my prophesies would be magnified a thousand times. I had tried to warn others; I should have warned myself.

If I had been depressed before, I was in deep despair now. When I realized I could never go back, I wanted to *really* kill myself. Even if I were acquitted of every crime I was accused of, I'd still spend the rest of my life in court, or worse, in front of a TV camera. And to risk never having this glorious solitude again? Forget it.

If I was being honest with myself—which I was trying to do more of lately—I knew deep down there had always been a possibility I'd never go back. Anyone who'd screwed up as badly as I had would jump at the chance to start over from scratch. I guess now the universe was setting it up so I could do just that.

So I wandered from town to town, dying my hair from blond to red to black, changing glasses and hats every few days. This is your new life, I told myself in the Texaco mirror.

Get used to it.

I enunciated the word *limbo* again and again, lingering over the long vowel sound: L-I-M-B-O. The nebulous place between two worlds. My new home.

Any options of returning to my "normal" life were now irrevocably gone. My whole amnesia story, Princeton, Peter's face as I walked through the kitchen door—history. My new vocation was spiritual hobo, never stopping long enough to make a connection. I had gone from a geek to a god to Richard-freaking-Kimble. Who knew?

Or did I have another choice?

Hiding behind the false identity of Larry had gotten me into this mess; was hiding behind Gil and Tom the answer now? A voice inside me said no. As painful as it would be, maybe it was time to face the music. To tell *my* side of the story. I could set up another anonymous Web site, of course, but wasn't that still begging the question? It was time to get back to basics; I bought an old manual typewriter and a ream of paper. No fancy graphics, simple, like a term paper—the thesis of my life. I worked on it for weeks, Larry's story—no, my story—pouring onto the pages. I hoped I could find someone to help me publish it without dealing with the Larry brouhaha.

I spent several days in the library researching local writers, disc jockeys, anyone who might listen to my version of these events. I made a list of people who were possibilities, then said a prayer someone would help me publish this thing. Not a prayer to Larry, just an old-fashioned is-anybody-out-there kind of prayer.

There's somebody out there, all right.

It's me.

Today I rose early and hitched a ride down Route 2. I had just finished typing the manuscript and wanted to celebrate. I also realized I'd never been to Walden Pond. The late autumn weather meant only a few courageous souls would brave the icy water. I hung out away from the other Nature lovers and watched, eventually diving into the chilly water myself. Like my new life, it took some getting used to, but once accepted, made me feel refreshed and renewed.

When the park closed, I made my way deeper into the woods.[75] Because it was illegal—and I was legally deceased—getting caught was risky indeed. After dark I reached the site where Thoreau's house had been. Several oaks and maples were thick with age; they would have been here when he wandered these woods too.

---

[75] Without a car, no possession gave me away.

Tomorrow I would approach a few writers and see if they'd help me tell my story. But for tonight, under the stars, I leaned against a pine tree and watched a great horned owl land above me. Its wingspan reached as wide as my arms; I gazed at it in wonder. And a feeling welled up inside me—you are free. And I realized, as crazy as the rest of the world seemed, I was.

If I got my story published, I'd actually be outing myself. The fact that I had something in common with betagold made me smile. Maybe finding common ground with the people we disagreed with was the first step to a real revolution. With this story behind me, I could concentrate on what has always been most important to me—contributing. But I didn't have to preach to a million people to move civilization forward; offering a hungry person a bowl of soup was contributing too. So was lending someone a pen, smiling at a frazzled waitress, letting the old man in front of me at the store take his time gathering his things.

I remembered an article I'd read during my anthropology phase. It described a "primitive" tribe with no doctor or shaman. Whenever anyone in the village was sick, he or she stood in the middle of a circle surrounded by their community. The person was asked, "What has been left unsaid?" People sometimes sat for hours, days, however long it took for them to draw the courage to say whatever they had been holding back, which was, of course, what was making them sick. In a culture with no doctor, the cure rate was 98 percent. I thought about that story now as I watched the owl. I had "died" with no last words, words that maybe could have saved my life. If I had told Beth how I felt about her from the beginning instead of having Larry seduce her like some kind of cyber-Cyrano de Bergerac. If I had really tried to discuss my anticonsumer views with Peter. Even more to the point, if I had told him that never in fifty lifetimes could I feel for Katherine what I felt for my mom, that her petty interests made a mockery of all the things Mom had held important. If I had told people straight out—I like you, you're fine, but COULD YOU PLEASE LEAVE ME ALONE FOR A WHILE, instead of hiding behind a screen name. All Larry's sermons came from his head. Maybe his heart—my heart—needed some airtime too.

Thoreau's spirit must have been protecting me, because I didn't hear or see a ranger all night. Slowly—with the clarity only a spiritual hibernation can bring—I realized my predicament was actually a blessing.

Life had given me another chance. This time around I could verbalize the unsaid things, cure myself before the villagers' very eyes. I had been trying to fix the outside world without fixing the inside one first—a giant mistake. How did a math and logic freak like me miss that one?

Through this cascade of thoughts, the owl remained above me. It sure wasn't Bloomingdale's, but I felt my mother's presence more than I ever had before. The thought of Mom and Henry David on some funky astral plane, talking about applying moisturizer and chopping wood made me laugh out loud. My body relaxed for the first time in weeks, and I knew my life would go on.

I *could* change the world.

I'd just start with me this time.

An easier or more difficult task?

I watched the moon and pondered the question till I fell asleep under the stars.

Epilogue

"Write the things which thou hast seen, and the things which are, and the things which shall be hereafter...."

REVELATION 1:19

"You will pardon some obscurities, for there are more secrets in my trade than in most men's, and yet not voluntarily kept, but inseparable from its very nature. I would gladly tell all that I know about it, and never paint 'No Admittance' on my gate."

Walden
HENRY DAVID THOREAU

My editor and I have our first disagreement about the book. She insists on publishing it under my name and listing it as fiction; I say it's Josh's story and should be packaged as nonfiction under his own name. Josh tells me to do whatever it takes to get the story out.

I originally told him I'd help him get his manuscript published because I thought it was the right thing to do. But now that the book is ready to go to press, I find myself wishing I had helped him more. My maternal instincts emerge, and I wonder if he's okay, if he has a place to stay and some food. I disapprove of Josh's pseudocide, and as a parent I go back and forth about calling Peter Swensen to tell him Josh is still alive. Peter's number sits on my desk, next to my John Lennon photo; in the end I decide it's a violation of Josh's privacy and don't. But I find myself hoping Peter will spot *The Gospel According to Larry* at some bookstore and make the connection for himself. I read a notice in the *Boston Globe* that he and Katherine recently married; I hope they find happiness together.

I did interview several people for this epilogue but decided not to include them. The person I really wanted to talk to was Beth, but she was organizing a rally for Third World workers' rights and wouldn't be back in the States until after the publication date. She has moved on from Larry, but not from their many causes.

I stop by the makeup counter at Bloomingdale's to see Marlene. "I miss my Joshie," she says. "No one comes to talk anymore." I buy a pale brown lipstick, sit on the padded stool, and wait. No one walking by says anything.

One Saturday afternoon, a woman appears at my door and introduces herself as Tracy Hawthorne.

I correct her. "Don't you mean betagold?"

She tells me she has a friend in the publishing industry who mentioned something about a new book coming out about Larry. I talk to her on the porch and don't invite her in. I tell her the rumor might be true.

"If he's still alive, I want to know," she says. "I *deserve* to know."

I want to tell her to get a life; instead I tell her I don't know anything about Larry. "You're asking the wrong person," I say. "I write fiction."

She climbs back into the waiting cab and drives off. I never see her again.

Larry's work continues to influence my life in different ways. Over the course of several weeks I clean out my house from top to bottom, eventually filling twenty-three bags with things my husband, son, and I don't need anymore. Although I hardly whittle our possessions down to seventy-five, I feel much lighter and less bogged down by junk. Whenever I go shopping—which is hardly ever—I ask myself if the item I am about to buy is worth adding to my life. Nine times out of ten it isn't, and I put it back on the shelf with a smile.

I also spend a little less time reading the tabloids at the check-out counters. I reexamine the reasons I'm a writer, begin an inner dialogue. Am I writing to express myself, to add ideas to the collective thought process? Or am I just out to sell books and get famous? I go back and forth, decide not to put my photo on the jacket of the book.

One day I go so far as to ride a bike—I have to borrow one—to the Sagamore Bridge. As I ride across, I am petrified, can't believe Josh even *pretended* to jump here. I think about the first time I met him, his quoting Thoreau while I unloaded groceries. I recall a line from Thoreau now: "You must live in the present, launch yourself on every wave, find your eternity in each moment." I realize I've gone as far with Larry as I can go. That it is now *my* turn to move on. I stand on the bridge with the wind behind me.

My husband thinks I seem preoccupied. "Usually when you finish a book, you're excited," he says. "Are you okay?"

I tell him I'm fine and tamp down the uneasy feeling that the book is done. The last time I see Josh, he is wearing a "MEAN PEOPLE SUCK" T-shirt and multiplying numbers on the napkin in front of him.

He pulls out a wad of papers from his jacket. "Listen to this," he says. "From Mother Teresa. 'We can do no great things, only small things with great love. . . . Do not wait for leaders; do it alone, person to person.'" His smile covers his entire face. "I love that."

He seems happier than anyone I've ever known.

Today my son and I walk through the Arboretum. By the time we reach the rhododendrons I know that I'm ready to begin my next book.

As we walk, I hear an airplane overhead and get a weird déjà vu about Larry. Wasn't there a scene in *his* story where he heard a plane in the sky? I shield my eyes from the sun and look up.

The plane methodically loops back and forth, leaving a trail of white vapor behind it. My son looks up and points to letters forming in the sky.

"What does it say?" he asks.

I read the words for him. "Larry — Come Back."

My son sounds out the letters, tries to read the words for himself. "Who's Larry?"

I tell him Larry was a boy I met once. He did yoga, loved numbers, and wanted more than anything to help change the world.

My son looks up at me and smiles. "You're making that up."

I shrug and head down the trail. After a few minutes, we sit under a cluster of pines—is that Larry's phrase or mine?—and stare up at nature's blue canvas. My son tries to read the words again, one letter at a time. I take a deep breath and join him, watching the word *Larry* recede into the blankness of the sky.

★ "Tashjian's gift for portraying bright adolescents with insight and humor reaches near perfection here."

—*School Library Journal*, Starred

THE GOSPEL ACCORDING TO LARRY

A READERS GUIDE

Janet Tashjian

1. In his quest to be antimaterialistic, Josh has just seventy-five possessions, including shirts, shoes, keys, books, CDs, and underwear. If you had to limit the things you own to seventy-five items, what would they be?

2. Josh states, "I've only wanted one thing my whole life—to contribute, to help make the world a better place . . . not with technology. . . but with ideas."(p.18) Is Josh true to his vision?

3. Is the way Josh/Larry manipulates his followers any different from the way the media, big business, or politicians manipulate the public?

4. Josh steals confidential documents from Peter's briefcase in order to attack the companies his stepfather represents. Is he right to do this? Does the end justify the means?

5. Paint a picture of Josh's character. Why is it that he has only one friend? Discuss his relationship with Beth. Do you think he would have created the Larry Web site if he had told Beth how he felt about her?

6. Discuss the ethics of spouting views on the Internet, or in any medium, under a false identity. Betagold claims that Larry is a coward for keeping his identity a secret. Do you agree? Or is Larry right to think that revealing who he is would detract from his message?

7. Discuss Josh's motivation for creating the Larry Web site. Is he being honest or is he just playing a game? He is disturbed by the magnitude of the response to his Web site and by the hero he becomes, but he does not close down the site. Why?

8. Josh is disillusioned by the reaction of the public once his identity is known. No one seems to be interested in his message—people are interested only in him as a celebrity. The producer of *20/20* tells him, "They want to know about you. . . . You're the story, just you. People want gossip; people want sizzle." (p.150) What does this tell you about how the media views the public? What happens when the sizzle fizzles?

9. Josh says that we feast on celebrities, caring for people who have no idea who we are. How do you feel about this? Should we care about the private lives of our favorite rock stars? If you were a celebrity, how would you handle fame?

10. "No offense, Josh, but this idealism thing is a phase, like so many others you've been through. . . . You don't have enough life experience. You don't know how the real world works yet."(p.154) How much of what Peter says to Josh is true, or is it as Josh responds, "Adults always say that to keep kids quiet"?

11. Some of Josh's actions might be considered unethical. Do you think anything Josh does is immoral? Is the writing of his story the solution for Josh, or is it just another way to avoid taking responsibility? How will Josh find peace? Is he on the right path?

12. Josh's/Larry's sermons rail against exploitation of third-world countries, celebrity worship, and the way big business manipulates our lives, to name a few issues. What are the things about society that you and your friends hope to change?

This guide was prepared by Clifford Wohl, educational consultant.

In her own words—
a conversation with

JANET TASHJIAN

Q: Authors are often besieged by aspiring writers to read their manuscripts. How often do you take the statement "I've got a great story that has to be told" seriously? What realistic advice do you give?

A: Whenever someone tells me they've got a story that has to be told, I take it *very* seriously. I think we all have amazing stories to tell, and the world needs to hear them. I'd go a step further and say it's our *obligation* to do so. (I'm talking about the kind of storytelling that fosters empathy, ideas, and discussion, not the trashy TV talk-show kind.) What I tell Josh in the book is true—"The best person to tell your story is you." Students need to be trained to communicate effectively by using fiction, debate, memoir, music, film, art, whatever. The spirit of each generation travels in stories; it's important to make sure teens have the tools to pass on their own narratives.

Q: You make references to several works of literature, among them *Walden, 1984, Catch-22,* Harry Potter, and *The Adventures of Tom Sawyer*. Beyond mentioning them in the novel, will you tell us a little about each of these books? Why are they important to you, and why would you recommend them to young adults?

A: I haven't read all the Harry Potter books but love the fact that millions of children are anticipating and devouring them. I look forward to enjoying them with my son. I read *Tom Sawyer* as a child; certainly the scene where he and Huck listen to their own funeral is one of the most memorable scenes in children's literature. Larry's dilemma echoes that scene.

One of the most gratifying things for me is hearing how many teens are reading Thoreau after finishing *Larry*. Walden Pond is not far from where I live; every time I walk those woods I imagine Henry David and his life of contemplation and work. His choice to live a simple, thoughtful existence is even more meaningful in the age of supertechnology we live in today. His books and essays should be required reading for all of us, no question.

I loved satire when I was young—still do—and *1984* and *Catch-22* are both excellent examples of how fiction can sound a warning bell about bureaucracy and technology run amok. *1984*—along with *Brave New World, Animal Farm,* and *Player Piano*—scared the life out of me when I first read them. (It's amazing what a good book can do.) Since then, I always wonder what big business and government are up to and run screaming the other way at the first whiff of anything resembling totalitarianism. *Catch-22* is a great example of how the world doesn't make sense no matter how hard you try to think it through. A very funny read. (Did you know the title was *Catch-18* up until the very last minute, when Heller's editor suggested changing it? I wonder if that title would have made such a lasting impression in the popular culture. . . .)

Q: Josh's/Larry's passions are about making the world a better place with the use of ideas. Do you think ideas can make a difference?

A: I certainly believe ideas can make a difference—but only if they're paired with action. It would be one thing for me to sit around spouting theories all day; but it's quite another thing to pick up a pen and write a book about them. I think we now live in an anti-idea culture. Intellectuals, academics, and activists are often put down as condescending or out of touch. But I don't think people are thinking *enough*—or at least about things that matter. I admire kids who actively work to make the world a better place; they keep me hopeful for our future.

Q: *The Gospel According to Larry* illustrates the power of the Internet as a worldwide mass communicator. Do you see this power as a danger to individual freedom? Is it different from other forms of mass communication?

A: I don't consider the Internet a danger to individual freedom; I see it as a democratic tool where people have access to enormous amounts of information. (Of course, not everyone has access to the Internet, and *that's* a problem.) For me, the Internet empowers people to hook up with others with similar interests or needs—support groups, medical information, continuing-ed classes, etc.—but we're still in the early stages. As with any technology, we won't discover the drawbacks until it's too late. (When they invented television, could anyone have predicted its use would be tied to obesity?) For example, I'm a huge fan of shared MP3 files, but I'm equally concerned with the infringement of artists' rights. These questions don't have simple answers; we need to sort them out as we go.

Q: You said that sometimes Josh's story seemed inspirational and other times, eerie and devoid of meaning. Are the extremes due to the fact that the story is being told by a seventeen-year-old? Teenagers often live on the edge.

A: I think we *all* live on the edge—on the edge of trying to understand the world, on the edge of discovering where we fit in. Like Josh's life, our own lives can be wondrous; a few minutes later, they can seem ludicrous and bizarre. I think we spend a lot of energy trying to make sense of it all, wondering why this, why that. I'm not sure those questions lend themselves to answers we can understand.

Q: Tell us more about the relationship between Josh and Beth. On the one hand, she has been his closest friend since they were kids, and on the other hand, she is unaware that he possesses only seventy-five things and she doesn't seem to recognize the items posted on the Larry Web site as things that Josh owns.

A: Part of that has to do with globalization—we all buy clothes from the same stores, food from the same restaurants, so your seventy-five possessions look the same as everyone else's. But the other part has to do with Josh's dilemma—he kept so much of his real life from Beth, she didn't know who he really was. I think people do that all the time; unfortunately the parts of ourselves we hide from others are usually the most interesting aspects of who we are.

Q: How do you deal with the issues of consumerism and big business? Are they personal concerns of yours?

A: I hardly watch TV and would rather be abducted by aliens than spend a day at the mall. Seriously, I think consumerism is one of the biggest problems facing our society today. Just because big business views us as consumers doesn't mean we have to see ourselves that way.

I don't have seventy-five possessions, but I don't buy anything without asking a few questions first: Is this item worth the energy required to maintain it, clean it, service it, store it? Most of the time, the answer is no and I end up not buying it.

Like Larry, my life works much better when it's not cluttered with a lot of stuff.

www.thegospelaccordingtolarry.com
Larry's official Web site

www.janettashjian.com
The author's own Web site

No Easy Answers
DONALD R. GALLO, EDITOR
0-440-41305-2
In response to the debate about teenagers'
moral standards (or lack of them), this
anthology contains sixteen stories about
teenagers who find themselves in situations
that test the strength of their character. There
are many tough choices. There are no easy
answers.

The Wave
TODD STRASSER
0-440-99371-7
What begins as a study of the forces that
fuel mass movements ends as a terrifying
experience that disrupts an entire school.
A dramatization of a true incident that
occurred at a California high school in 1969.

Teen Angst? Naaah ...
NED VIZZINI
0-440-23767-X
Ned Vizzini writes about the weird, funny,
and sometimes mortifying moments that
made up his teen years. With wit, irony, and
honesty, *Teen Angst? Naaah ...* invites you
into his world of school, parents, street
people, rock bands, friends, fame, camp,
sex (sort of), Cancún (almost), prom, beer,
Nintendo, the cool (and almost cool),
and more.

Tribes
ARTHUR SLADE
0-385-73003-9
From an award-winning Canadian author
comes a brilliant, quirky story about the
bizarre culture known as high school.
Rituals, strange tribes, and transitional
ceremonies in Grade Twelve teach Percy a lot
about the world around him and even more
about himself.

Heaven Eyes
DAVID ALMOND
0-440-22910-3

Erin Law and her friends in the orphanage are labeled Damaged Children. They run away one night, traveling downriver on a raft. What they find on their journey is stranger than you can imagine.

Kit's Wilderness
DAVID ALMOND
0-440-41605-1

Kit Watson and John Askew look for the childhood ghosts of their long-gone ancestors in the mines of Stoneygate.

Skellig
DAVID ALMOND
0-440-22908-1

Michael feels helpless because of his baby sister's illness, until he meets a creature called Skellig.

Becoming Mary Mehan: Two Novels
JENNIFER ARMSTRONG
0-440-22961-8

Set against the events of the American Civil War,
The Dreams of Mairhe Mehan depicts an
Irish immigrant girl and her family, struggling to find their place in the war-torn country.
Mary Mehan Awake takes up Mary's story after the war, when she must begin a journey of renewal.

Forgotten Fire
ADAM BAGDASARIAN
0-440-22917-0

In 1915, Vahan Kenderian is living a life of privilege when his world is shattered by the Turkish-Armenian war.

The Rag and Bone Shop
ROBERT CORMIER
0-440-22971-5

A seven-year-old girl is brutally murdered. A twelve-year-old boy named Jason was the last person to see her alive—except, of course, for the killer. Unless *Jason* is the killer.

When Zachary Beaver Came to Town
KIMBERLY WILLIS HOLT
0-440-23841-2

Nothing ever happens in Toby's small Texas town. Nothing much, that is, until this summer full of big changes. The sleepy town is about to get a jolt with the arrival of Zachary Beaver, billed as the fattest boy in the world. Toby is in for a summer unlike any other, a summer sure to change his life.

Ghost Boy
IAIN LAWRENCE
0-440-41668-X

Fourteen-year-old Harold Kline is an albino—an outcast. When the circus comes to town, Harold runs off to join it in hopes of discovering who he is and what he wants in life. Is he a circus freak or just a normal guy?

Lord of the Nutcracker Men
IAIN LAWRENCE
0-440-41812-7

In 1914, Johnny's father leaves England to fight the Germans in France. With each carved wooden soldier he sends home, the brutality of war becomes more apparent. Soon Johnny fears that his war games foretell real battles and that he controls his father's fate.

Gathering Blue

LOIS LOWRY

0-440-22949-9

Lamed and suddenly orphaned, Kira is mysteriously taken to live in the palatial Council Edifice, where she is expected to use her gifts as a weaver to do the bidding of the all-powerful Guardians.

The Giver

LOIS LOWRY

0-440-23768-8

Jonas's world is perfect. Everything is under control. There is no war or fear or pain. There are no choices, until Jonas is given an opportunity that will change his world forever.

Shades of Simon Gray

JOYCE MCDONALD

0-440-22804-2

Simon is the ideal teenager—smart, reliable, hardworking, trustworthy. Or is he? After Simon's car crashes into a tree and he slips into a coma, another portrait of him begins to emerge.

Both Sides Now

RUTH PENNEBAKER

0-440-22933-2

A compelling look at breast cancer through the eyes of a mother and daughter. Liza must learn a few life lessons from her mother, Rebecca, about the power of family.

Her Father's Daughter

MOLLIE POUPENEY

0-440-22879-4

As she matures from a feisty tomboy of seven to a spirited young woman of fourteen, Maggie discovers that the only constant in her life of endless new homes and new faces is her ever-emerging sense of herself.

The Baboon King
ANTON QUINTANA
0-440-22907-3

Neither Morengáru's father's Masai tribe nor his mother's
Kikuyu tribe accepts him. Banished from both tribes,
Morengáru encounters a baboon troop and faces a fight
with the simian king.

Holes
LOUIS SACHAR
0-440-22859-X

Stanley has been unjustly sent to a boys' detention
center, Camp Green Lake. But there's more than
character improvement going on at the camp—the
warden is looking for something.

The Gospel According to Larry
JANET TASHJIAN
0-440-23792-0

Josh Swensen's virtual alter ego, Larry, becomes a huge
media sensation. While it seems as if the whole world is
trying to figure out Larry's true identity, Josh feels
trapped inside his own creation.

Memories of Summer
RUTH WHITE
0-440-22921-9

In 1955, thirteen-year-old Lyric describes her older sister
Summer's descent into mental illness, telling Summer's
story with humor, courage, and love.